FOREVER THE COLOURS

Forever the Colours

THAMES RIVER PRESS
An imprint of Wimbledon Publishing Company Limited (WPC)
Another imprint of WPC is Anthem Press (www.anthempress.com)
First published in the United Kingdom in 2013 by
THAMES RIVER PRESS
75–76 Blackfriars Road
London SE1 8HA

www.thamesriverpress.com

A CIP record for this book is available from the British Library.

ISBN 978-1-78308-163-9

This title is also available as an eBook

FOREVER THE COLOURS

RICHARD THOMAS

THAMES RIVER PRESS

For my father the storyteller.
My inspiration.

"On the 30th October [1878] the ultimatum was despatched to Sher Ali, informing him that, unless his acceptance of the conditions were received by the Viceroy not later than the 20th November, he would be treated by the British Government as a declared enemy."

—Field Marshal Lord Roberts, 1897

"The battle is now joined on many fronts. We will not waver, we will not tire, we will not falter, and we will not fail. Peace and freedom will prevail."

—George W. Bush, 2001

Prologue

It was just out of reach, no more than a hand span away. His fingers desperately clawed at the sand and gravel, fingernails tearing and ripping off. With a desperation made of pure will-power, he levered his body forward using his elbows as pivots and managed another couple of inches towards his target. 'Hail Mary, full of grace, Hail Mary, full of grace,' he choked in between sobbing breaths.

He reached out and winced at the sudden electrifying pain that exploded between his shoulder blades. Once again he reached back to try and remove the object that had been so cruelly punched into his back, but found he couldn't. His legs were useless; he hadn't felt them for some time now, and they were dragging along behind like unwanted passengers. He tried to take a breath but only managed a lung full of sand and dirt; he coughed and nearly fainted with the pain.

It was close now. His vision was dimming, the day turning to twilight, but through the tears he could see just how close it was. One more push and he would be there. He lifted himself again, shakily onto his elbows, his strength ebbing swiftly, and he found he could hardly keep his head up. 'Hail Mary, full of grace,' he pulled again, gritting his teeth at the agony emanating from his body. He slumped down, face resting in the dirt. He was going; he knew he didn't have long. He listened to the sounds around him, the screaming and laughing. He was taken back to May Day celebrations: the screaming boys and girls, whirling around the maypole on the village green, good food, ale, games and Annie. He would miss Annie.

He lifted his head weakly. There it was, right there in front of him. He pushed his hand out toward it, closer, closer. His fingers touched the material. He caressed it, grabbed it in his fist; relief washed over him and he smiled despite the pain. He gently pulled the once-colourful cloth toward him. It slipped, so he gripped it harder; it was difficult as it was wet, covered in warm butter, he thought.

Not far now. If he could just rest his head on it, he was sure he would feel better. It stopped, and found he couldn't move it. A curious pain, a new pain, crept up from his fist. What now, he thought, and looked to find his fingers being broken and crushed by a sandaled foot. It was grinding and pushing his broken bones into the dirt. He sobbed, not for the pain, but for the loss of the precious article he had given his last breaths trying to reach.

'Gawd help me.'

The soldier didn't feel a thing as the blade swooped down and plunged into the back of his neck...

Chapter 1

Shaman

Sweat!

He could feel it sliding down his right temple and down his cheek, to disappear inside his collar, which was already soaked with body oils. He sniffed and found he was starting to smell like his dog's bed blanket. What a fucking dump! Thomas 'Tommy' Evans was twenty-four years of age, a carpenter's son and a soldier, and the last place he wanted to be at that moment was where he actually found himself. There wasn't one redeeming feature about it, and the words hot, dusty, shit-smelling, fly-infested and pig sty sprung to mind. He had never gotten used to the smell of cow or goat shit, or whatever the hell shit it was; it stank. *They* seemed to use it for a wide variety of things. "The main one," he thought,"is building their homes. And what makes it worse are the flies. Millions of sodding flies, big, fat, bloated flies."

Why the hell anybody wanted to live in a shithole like this, let alone fight over it, was beyond his reasoning. He could have been in Germany or Canada or somewhere like that, getting pissed and wooing the local females with his god-like qualities. But no, here he was, living it up in downtown fuck all!

'Why do I have to be a bloody target for em? Bastards,' he mumbled. He slapped at a fly on his neck for what he thought was the hundredth time – and missed again. 'Bastards,' he said, again, a little too loudly.

'Eh, shut it dickhead,' whispered a sneering voice that sounded as though it was full of phlegm. 'You wanna get us all killed or what?'

The voice belonged to Sergeant Andy "the Arsehole" Adams (though the arsehole in question didn't know that was one of the loving names his platoon had given him). He was probably the most disliked soldier in her Majesty's own Fusiliers. 6', 6'1", he was broad in the shoulder, with a face that spoke of a link to the lost one, knuckles that dragged on the floor and an all-around nasty piece of work; and it also didn't help that he had the broadest scouse accent ever.

'Sorry Sar'nt,' Tommy replied ever so quietly. 'I'm being eaten alive. Have you seen how fat these fuckers are with my blood?' Truth be told, he wanted to tell Adams to poke it right up his fat Neanderthal arse, but he was going for his first stripe when he got back, so thought better of it.

'Youll be sorry when I come over there and crack yer head for ya,' spat Adams.

Tommy was lying behind a rough, broken wall made of dried cow or goat shit – Yes, he was sure that was what they were made of – in an Afghan village with a name he couldn't even pronounce. The usual day's events included searching for ragheads with guns, or insurgents as *they* are called on the news, oh, and not getting any of your body parts blown off by IEDs, especially the most valuable bit! He didn't call it the Kaiser for nothing.

With Adams in charge, Tommy's section was covering this part of the village, and the rest of the platoon was with Lieutenant Richard Dashwood at the north end.

'How long we gotta sit here for, Sar'nt?' asked Jacko, in his Peckham accent.

''Til I say we can fucking move, shithouse. Now shut it,' was the curt reply.

Tommy couldn 't help but chuckle, quietly of course, because although he couldn't see Jacko, he knew he would be mouthing all sorts of silent colourful replies. To say that Jacko hated Adams was probably an understatement. He despised him. Most did, but make no mistake, Adams was a true soldier, and a leader to some extent. It's just that, well, he was an arsehole!

After fifteen minutes of watching the cluster of mud huts for anything a little more dangerous than women and children going about their daily lives, Adams stood and bellowed at the section to move out and start the search of the area.

This was a massive relief for Tommy; just to be moving was a release from the blood suckers, and, moving up with Jacko on his left, he started towards the nearest hut. He looked sideways at Jacko, who had an angry expression on his face.

'What a twat,' said Jacko after a few moments.

'You can say that again,' replied Tommy.

'What a twat.'

Tommy smiled. He had been working with Lance Corporal Paul 'Jacko' Jackson for the best part of three years now. This was their second tour of Afghanistan and they were close friends. The loss of comrades on their first tour had built a strong bond between a lot of the lads, and especially between these two; they almost always stuck together when on patrol and today was no different. Tommy and Jacko moved with the confidence built on solid friendship, although Jacko had tested that friendship on quite a few occasions, the last being the time they had both been on leave and had pulled a couple of birds down the local pub.

The night had gone well and had ended up with Tommy and this girl, over the bonnet of a VW Passat, up an alley. What Tommy didn't know, but Jacko did, was that the girl he was entertaining, the sister of Jacko's interest, was in fact the wife of Sergeant Andrew Adams. Well, he did find out, as he lay slumped on top of her, breathing like he'd just ran a marathon, while Sergeant Adams bellowed in the road adjoining the alley, drunk, and looking for that 'fucking old slapper.' Tommy had been confused as to why the girl had shoved him off and frantically started to yank her knickers back up. The statement, 'Fuck it, that's my husband,' had haunted Tommy ever since, but what made it worse was when Jacko had come hurtling down the alley whooping like a school girl, went flying past Tommy and shouted, 'Fucking leg it!' Tommy had taken off after him, desperately trying to put away the now fear-shrunken Kaiser into his pants whilst simultaneously attempting to pull his trousers up. A couple of miles down the road, with a few cuts and bruises from all the short cuts Jacko led them through, they were back at the base; and Jacko could still hardly breathe for all the laughing he was doing. It had been the rumour ever since, and the main joke in the platoon, that the Sergeant's wife had a new taste for German salami!

Adam's voice echoed around the village, 'Don't forget lads, hearts and minds, hearts and minds; we need these fuckers to love us, long time.'

'Bleedin' 'ell, is he talkin' about us or the natives?'

'Come on Jacko, you know you love him deep down.'

'Yeah, about as much as I love having the squits.'

After about half an hour of checking dried mud-shit dwellings and animal stalls, and attempting to talk with the locals – which was pretty hard considering most of them didn't want the soldiers there, and the endless children begged for chocolate or sweets – the section were told to take a ten-minute break before moving on to the next village, about two kilometres away. The two friends found a bit of shade below one of the endless cow-goat shite walls and dug out their canteens. Slaking his thirst, Tommy then gave the local kids a packet of Polo mints to share and politely told them to piss off. He felt sorry for these kids. Well, most of them, anyway; they certainly had nothing. Sometimes, though, he had to be wary of them. If they weren't spotting for the insurgents, they were hiding them, though usually under duress.

'I can't stand much more of that twat, you know, mate, and if he calls me shithouse once more, I swear to God, I'm gonna kick his head in.'

'You shouldn't let him get to you, Jacko; he's just a bully. I just let it wash over me, mate, it's just bravado bullshit, that's all. Just try and picture me and his missus over the bonnet of that Passat.'

'Yeah, I know.' Jacko's smile didn't last. 'But the longer this tour goes on the more wound up I get, and I reckon I'm gonna end up knocking him out.' He laid his helmeted head back against the wall and sighed. 'What we doing here, Tommy, eh? Nobody wants this place, apart from the smackheads, anyway, and no bleedin' army has ever won here.' He looked at his friend. 'It's a shithole and a total waste of time.'

Tommy smiled. 'Mate, we're freeing these people from the Taliban; al-Qaeda, the muja-whatyamacallits, and all those other mad mozzy bastards. We're the British Army, mate, freeing the world, protecting the innocent. Queen, country, honour, the regiment and all that jazz.'

'The regiment? What, some poxy colours? You might wanna die for the flag, Tommy, but I fuckin' don't.' Jacko spat angrily into the sand at his boots.

'I didn't mean it like that, mate. Calm down, eh.'

Jacko sighed again and nodded to Tommy. 'I'm sorry, mate, I just have a real lousy feeling this time around, like it's gonna go properly tits up.'

'Mate, we all think that at some point, it's normal. Listen, we get this tour out the way and we fuck off home.'

'Yeah, but this time feels different…like something's gonna happen.' He sighed again and sat forward, took his helmet off and poured water from his canteen over his head. 'Bollocks, I sound like a right nut job.' He looked at Tommy with a wry smile. 'You know what, mate, me and her sister could see your arse pumping away like a jackhammer down that alley.'

Tommy was about to reply when they heard raised voices coming from the back of one of the dwellings on the opposite side of the road. And one of the raised voices was that of Adams himself.

'That don't sound too brilliant, does it, mucka?' said Jacko as he put his helmet back on and started to get to his feet. 'Think we best go see, eh?'

They stood, checked their rifles and hurried across the dusty road, covering each other at all times, and moved around a building that was probably the biggest in the village. They found a small enclosure with a few chickens in it – well, they looked like chickens, just more bone that meat – and a door to the rear of the property. They both went to different sides of the doorway, listening, and, after a moment or two, and feeling safe to enter, Jacko used hand signals to indicate that Tommy should enter first, with Jacko, rifle raised, following close behind.

To say the circumstances in which the two friends found themselves were awkward would possibly demean the situation. It was extreme shit. Adams was there, towering over an old white-bearded bloke, his fist pressed against the man's sunken cheek, and a young Afghan was doing a terrific impression of a dying fly while managing to piss blood all over somebody's prayer mat from a split lip. He looked at Tommy with pleading eyes.

The Sergeant was attempting to talk native, in a broad scouse accent.

'You is fucking Taliban,' he screeched. 'Where are the fucking boom booms?'

By 'boom booms', it was assumed he was asking where the IEDs were hidden. Improvised Explosive Devices, scourge of the Allied troops, or rather the British, Commonwealth and US troops. The closest some of our European friends got to the action was a martini and a blow job from some dusky-skinned sexbomb.

To the left of Adams was Private Bell, aka 'Dinga', who was pissing himself with laughter. To say that Dinga was dislikeable was probably unfair; he was an arse-kisser of the best sort and had attached himself to Adams's arse like a limpet. You could not speak about anything noteworthy in front of Dinga for fear of it getting back to the Sergeant. Plus he was a ginger, and the one thing Tommy knew for sure was that gingers were a different breed and could not, under any circumstances, be trusted.

There was also the problem of not being able to understand Dinga, as he was a foreigner, you see, from an exotic place called Newcastle. In fact, just as Tommy had entered the building, he heard Dinga say;

'Wy man, gi it fuckin te im, da fuckin oold twet.'

Which, roughly translated, probably meant, 'I say old boy, now don't make it hard on yourself.'

He managed to say this while flicking spit all over the old man.

Given the size of Adams, and the temper he was in, the old geezer, with the imposing Santa beard and skin like leather, was doing an admirable job of not shitting himself; he was just smiling benignly back at the hulking Sergeant, which was winding him up even more. The old man looked at Tommy and held his gaze for a few moments. What Tommy felt right then, he could not explain: understanding, maybe sorrow. And not for himself.

'I'm not gonna ask you again, Abdul,' exploded Adams. 'I know you can speaky de English, shithouse.'

Tommy attempted to defuse the situation. 'What's up, Sar'nt,' he asked, in a pleasant voice, though he knew only too well the methods of questioning Adams used, especially when he was convinced the person he was talking to was related to the Bin Liner himself. Tommy smiled at the old man, to try and reassure him, and the old man smiled back.

'I am asking this wrinkled old fart, lad, where he has hidden those nasty little things that separate your legs from your body.' He walked over to Tommy and Jacko and put his nose tip-to-tip with Tommy's. The hatred in Adams's eyes right then confirmed to Tommy that the Sergeant knew he had bumped his wife. 'Now while me and Dinga sort this out,' he growled, 'you and your mate shithouse there, go and sweep the rest of the buildings, savvy? Now, chop chop.' And with that he turned and walked back to the old man, who was still on his knees, and fetched a hard slap to his leathery cheek.

Weak as he knew he could sometimes be, Tommy turned, grabbed Jacko's arm and pulled him through the doorway back into the street. They stood facing each other in the heat and dust, and listened as another slap resounded through the doorway, accompanied by a muffled squeal, which was possibly Dinga laying the boot into the young Afghan.

Tommy was breathing hard. What he had just witnessed wasn't nice and he wished he were someplace else. 'You alright, Jacko? You look pale,' Tommy said with concern, because Jacko had indeed lost all colour in his face. 'Jacko, are you alright?'

Jacko was staring straight into Tommy's eyes, though not seeming to see him, and his lips were trembling slightly. 'I can't leave it like this, Tommy,' Jacko said. 'We can't leave that poor old bastard in there with those fuckers. They'll kill him.'

SLAP!

Jacko shivered.

'What exactly do you think we can do? Oh, I know! We'll just walk right in there and ask him to stop, eh? Get a fucking grip, mate, you can't touch him. We're losing too many guys out in this shithole. Do you think the brass are gonna worry about one old man and a kid? Just do your job, don't get killed and go home. Don't try to be a fucking hero.'

SLAP!

'I can't take this, mate. I'm gonna have him, sorry.' And with that he turned round to re-enter the building.

Tommy, seeing his friend was about to pop, jumped in front of him and placed a hand on his chest. 'Hang on, hang on, stop, wait. Listen, you fucking idiot, we do it our way and we survive.'

He was shoved to the side as Jacko stormed through the door.

'Oh, sod it!' he said, and quickly followed behind.

As Tommy entered, his friend was nose-to-nose with Dinga, who, with a smirk on his face, had stepped in front of Adams and squared up to Jacko.

'Wots ya fuc'in problem meet?' Dinga said to Jacko. 'If ye fuc'in want sum, am reet ear.'

Tommy quickly surveyed the scene. The old man was pushing himself up off the floor.

'So what you two love birds back for then, eh?' said the Arsehole. 'Well??? Oh, it's like that is it, a fuckin' rescue mission. Well why don't ya piss off and mind ya fuckin' business?' Adams waited for any reaction from the two friends. 'Nothing to say, no? Didn't think so.' As he ended this sentence, he pulled back to strike the old man again, and the man, already bleeding from the nose, was still looking him straight in the eye, smiling.

So it was then that Tommy, who wasn't the one threatening to pop, stepped in.

Before anyone knew what was happening, Tommy had covered the prayer rug in two strides and placed himself in front of the old man as Adams's backhand connected with his right temple. He staggered slightly and saw little lights dancing in front of his eyes, but he didn't go down. After this, it all became rather chaotic. Jacko's helmeted forehead connected with Dinga's nose and mouth just as he was about to utter another incomprehensible mouthful, and a second later Tommy's right boot went into the ascent and squeezed Adams's left testicle against his inner thigh. The noise he made as he dropped to his knees was like air escaping from a punctured inner tube. On his way down he was rewarded with a knee to the forehead, which flicked his head back, and he tumbled onto his arse. Meanwhile Jacko was attempting to remould Dinga's Playdough face with his right fist into something more attractive to the animal kingdom.

Luckily for the two friends, a few of the platoon, on hearing the raised voices, entered the room as the scene was reaching its climax, and managed to jump on the two before they could seriously put the boot in. With both of them now restrained, Adams attempted, in a crab like fashion, to get out of the door, whilst making veiled threats of death at Tommy. But nobody was taking him seriously when he was talking like Joe Pasquale, so he was promptly ignored.

'Hthou futhin nick'ed, ye broork thme futhin nors ye naa,' was all anybody could make out of the ramblings of Dinga as he staggered after the Sergeant.

It all went quiet for a few moments.

'Well, that's you two fucked when we get back to camp, boys,' said the thickset lad called Terry, from Coventry. 'The Arsehole ain't gonna let this one go.'

'Fuck him, he's just a bully, him and that fucking dickhead Bell. He's been pushing us all around for too long, and you lot would have done the same given the chance.'

'Wanting and doing are totally feckin' different, ye eejits,' drawled Private Kerr, from Northern Ireland who everybody called Wayne even though his first name was Ian. 'We would all love to kick the shite outta those two, but rules is rules and all dat.'

With that statement left hanging in the air, the other soldiers turned and went out the door, leaving the Tommy and Jacko alone.

Tommy was gutted. 'Oh shit, oh shit, oh shit,' he kept saying, over and over. 'How the hell did that happen? Jesus Christ, we're finished, Jacko, it's all over. Shit, bollocks, twat.'

Tommy slumped onto an old crate and hung his head in his hands, knowing without a doubt that his career was over, as was Jacko's. As soon as he could manage, Adams would report to the Lieutenant, who in turn would report to the CO back at the base. Before anyone could say 'court martial', they would be on their way home and to the nearest unemployment office.

The old man was kneeling on his rug and chattering away in Pashto to the young Afghan, whose nose was now swelling, courtesy of Dinga, and was gesturing towards Tommy.

'My grandpa wishes to thank you, soldier, for helping him,' said the young Afghan.

'Yeah, well, tell him bollocks in buggi buggi 'cos that's me job gone down the swanee, mate,' replied Tommy.

Unperturbed, the young man continued translating into English what the old man was saying. 'My grandpa says that your journey is about to be cut short, but he will help.' The old man moved closer to Tommy and held out both his hands toward him.

'What's he gonna do, give him a job?' said Jacko, who was standing by the door.

Tommy stood and stepped backwards involuntarily. He didn't know what it was about this guy, but he gave him the creeps. He looked about a hundred years old.

The old man continued gesturing to Tommy to take his hands. 'What's 'e bloody after, money or what?' he said to the young Afghan. He tried to sound confident, but he couldn't understand why he was so spooked. It's his eyes, he thought, bright blue and piercing.

The old man continued to chatter on, looking at Tommy and gesturing and doing little hand signals.

'My grandfather says a real friend is one who takes the hand of his friend in times of distress and helplessness. He says he will guide you through what will be.'

The old man fell silent and gave Tommy a beatific smile.

Softening, Tommy sighed and held out his hand for the old man, though it was shaking slightly. The old man gripped the outstretched hand in both of his, which were surprisingly hot and strong, and, again speaking in Pashto, he stared straight into Tommy's eyes. These were not the eyes of an old man any more. There was fire in them, and passion, a knowing look that had seen much, travelled far and could tell many a story.

'My grandpa says you will travel far but will not move. You will lose but will gain much more. He also says do not despair, for there is a path to even the tallest mountain. Look for him on your journey and your return.'

Tommy pulled his hand back. It felt as though an electric shock had gone through him. He tried to sound cocky again.

'My return? Ha, I don't think so, mate. I'll be down the local job centre. But anyhow, say thanks for the advice.'

With that, he turned to Jacko and they both tumbled out into the sunlight.

Chapter 2
Contact

S ome say that if literacy rates were measured by a nation's proverbs and poetry, Afghanistan would be one of the most literate countries on earth. But to Private Tommy Evans, walking along a dusty road with his mate Jacko to rejoin the patrol, what the old man had said made about as much sense as Dinga in his Geordie patwa. Jacko was staring at his feet as he walked, like a condemned man, and as he glanced up under his helmet, he noticed all the lads gathered round Dinga and Adams. A medic was taking a look at Dinga's nose while Adams was squatting about five paces away from everybody else and looking a little red in the face. Well, more purple, really.

'What's gonna happen, mucka, do ya think?' Jacko mumbled under his breath.

'Well, I say we go over and pretend nothing happened, and perhaps everyone will forget we were ever here. What do you think's gonna bloody happen, you dickhead?' seethed Tommy under his breath 'The CO will have us out as soon as look at us.'

Jacko looked despondent. 'I'm sorry, mate, I couldn't help it, and I couldn't stand by and watch. Or listen even.'

'Oh crap, don't look now, Dashwood's walking up the street.'

Jacko looked beyond the group to where Tommy indicated. The Lieutenant and his section were indeed walking up the street, and he had a face like thunder. Walking next to him was one of the lads who had witnessed what happened in the house; he must have skipped to the other side of the village to report what had occurred.

'Bollocks, he looks happy.'

'Well, that's that then. We're in a world of shit now, mucka,' whispered Jacko. 'The Dick will go by the book on this one.' The Dick was the name some of the lads used for Dashwood, a shortened version of his first name – and because he is one.

'Just keep your gob closed and see where the wind's blowing,' whispered Tommy. 'We can try and figure out what to say back at base. Maybe we can get some witnesses to say what those wankers were doing back there.'

They reached the group just as the other section did. Before anybody could say anything, Dashwood pointed and said, in a decidedly clipped tone, 'Sergeant Adams, a word if you please,' and then moved to a small walled-off area about twenty feet away. Adams stood and, after a bit of wheezing, looked at the two friends, smirked and lumbered off after the Lieutenant with a slight limp.

All eyes were on Tommy and Jacko, some with pity, some with admiration, some non-committal. The big, strapping lad Terry moved over to them.

'Best not say anything here, lads, and wait till you get back to base. You know, get your story straight and all that.' Terry dipped his head and moved back to the group, and on his way accidentally tripped and stood on Dinga's hand. The screech was quite feminine sounding.

The two friends moved away and crouched down behind a wall to get some shade. Tommy was starting to feel the pressure as the minutes ticked by. *It's strange,*' he thought, *how your comrades give you a wide berth when you're in the shit*. He looked over at Jacko and was rewarded with the same downtrodden look he himself wore.

'Oh well, mucka. I always wanted to be a florist anyway,' Jacko said with a smile.

'Oh, you're dead funny, mate. You know what, I can hardly breathe with all fun I'm having.' Tommy stood suddenly, his anger building. 'How many times have you got us in the shit now, eh? Once, twice, a thousand – I've lost count, you twat.' He looked up at the sky and sighed. 'Well, you've done it this time, for both of us.' He turned and moved away a couple of feet.

Jacko looked crestfallen but didn't get a chance to say anything because Dashwood, the Sergeant in his wake, started to make his way back to the group. Jacko jumped to his feet and stood next to Tommy, looking as if he were on a parade ground.

'Permission to speak, sir,' he said as the Lieutenant drew closer.

'Denied,' stated Dashwood matter-of-factly. 'Right, gentlemen, we will move on and make a sweep of the next village.' He stopped and consulted a map that one of his section had supplied out of thin air, and after some frowning and pursing of lips, he looked up.

'Right, I want the same again as we move across those fields,' he said, indicating by pointing. 'This time I will take the Sergeant's section, Smythers and Daniels will go with Sergeant Adams, and you two,' he looked directly at Tommy and Jacko, 'will be coming with me.'

'Yes sir,' came the booming reply.

'We will be moving in a northerly direction, and I want you and your section to move up the east side of the field. Do it by the book and take it steady and keep in contact.'

'Sir.'

Still consulting his map, he said, 'Right. It is approximately two kilometres to the next village and it's quite a large field with lots of scrub, so there is the possibility we will lose sight of one another. Maintain radio contact at all times.'

Adams was rolling his eyes as Dashwood continued.

'If you make contact before me, hunker down and wait until we move up, clear?'

'As crystal, sir.'

He folded the map away and tucked it into his top pocket, 'Right, gentlemen, let's be about our business, and remember to keep your bloody eyes open. Nobody wants any surprises. Alright, marvellous.'

With that, Adams and his section moved out, first heading towards the end of the street before turning north and entering the fields. Dinga tried to smile at the two friends but his fast-swelling mouth just looked like a cat's arse. He gave them the bird instead and hurried off after Adams.

As the Lieutenant moved off, he called Tommy and Jacko to his side. When they had trotted up to him and continued at a brisk pace towards their end of the village he said, 'Gentlemen, I do not care for this sort of behaviour and I will not stand for it, do you hear? This sort of thing is unbecoming a British soldier.' He took a deep breath and continued in a softer tone, 'For the love of God, haven't we enough problems with the bloody enemy trying to destroy us, without you two throwing your bloody fists around. I cannot have my soldiers behaving like, well, like, I don't know, the bloody *Yanks* or something.'

'Sir, it was my fault,' blurted Jacko, 'Tommy had nothing to do with it, he was just trying to break it up and…'

'Shut up, Jackson,' warned Dashwood. 'If I wanted to hear your version of events, believe you me I would have asked for them.'

'But sir…'

'Enough. You can recount your epic tale to the old man after I give him my report on what Sergeant Adams told me. In the meantime, shut up.' He stopped and took a deep breath. 'Right here we are. You and Evans will take point and keep your bloody eyes peeled, all right? Do not think, gentlemen. Do. Marvellous.' He waved his hands like he was shooing away birds, indicating the direction he wanted them to go.

Tommy and Jacko looked at each other for a moment and then started across the field. Keeping about fifteen feet apart, with Jacko slightly in front, they flicked their eyes between scanning the terrain ahead and looking at the ground. Getting picked off by a Taliban sniper or getting blown to bits standing on an IED was not a comfortable thought to either of them, but they were professionals and they knew their business. And they had done this many, many times before.

It was hard going. The sun was hot and the air fetid, and how anyone could grow crops in this lifeless soil was beyond Tommy's understanding. Unless, of course, it was a particular type of crop that could thrive in poor soils and under full sun, the kind of crop that, when cultivated, made a lot of money on the streets of the world's cities.

After half an hour, and about a third of the way across the first of two fields, Jacko's fist went into the air. He crouched down, quickly followed by the rest of the section.

'What you got, Jacko?' said Tommy.

Into his radio Jacko said, 'Possible enemy contact approximately two-hundred metres to front. Over.'

Tommy looked through the scope of his SA80 rifle, slowly panning around to focus on the end of the field.

'What have you got, Lance Corporal? Over.' Dashwood's voice came over the radio net.

'Unknown, sir. Reflection of some kind, possibly scope. Over.'

'Do you see anything now? Over.'

'Standby,' Jacko said. He scanned around the brush and plough furrows where he thought he had seen the reflection. After thirty seconds he replied, 'That's a negative. Over.'

Dashwood, who was perhaps forty metres behind the two on point, bit his lip, thinking. After a moment, he radioed Adams and asked how far his section was across the field, to which he was told a little further on than his own. They had also gone to ground after Jacko's transmission. The Sergeant had Private Daniels on point and promptly contacted him by radio to see if he had any contact ahead.

'Err...that's a negative, I think. Over,' replied Daniels, an eighteen-year-old on his first tour, who was a little skittish.

'Daniels, do you see any movement from the front, anything?'

'I don't see any movement to front Sar'nt. Over.'

Adams, to his credit, moved up to Daniels' position and checked the front with his scope. After about twenty seconds he keyed his mike, 'That's a negative on forward contact, I think shi— Jackson's seeing things. Over.' Adams chuckled to himself over this, and what made it funnier for him was the fact that they could see each other quite well. The Sergeant waved to Jacko, who promptly replied by giving him the bird.

'Twat,' said Jacko to no one in particular. But Tommy had heard him.

'You can say that again.'

'Twat.' They both looked at each other and started to laugh.

'Lance Corporal Jackson,' thundered Dashwood's voice from behind, 'If it's that funny, why don't you share it with the rest of us.'

'Sorry sir, coughing. Permission to advance, sir?'

'Well, get a bloody move on then, or we will be out here all bloody night at this rate,' screeched Dashwood.

'Yes, sir.'

With that, the two friends started forward again. After about another five minutes, Tommy took a quick look to his right, past Jacko, and saw that Adams's point man Daniels had stopped, staring ahead. *What's got him spooked?* he thought. Suddenly the lad was trying to raise his rifle and key his mike at the same time. But before he could do either, young Daniels managed to throw himself backwards, landing on his back. For a split second Tommy was confused as to why he would have done this. But then he heard the report of a rifle, a loud one at that.

CRACK.

Tommy, Jacko and the rest of the platoon went face down in the dust, and Tommy and Jacko brought their rifles to bear on where they thought the shot might have come from.

'Jacko, see anything?' shouted Tommy.

'Nothing, fuck all,' screamed Jacko. 'Oh shit! Daniels has been hit.' From his dusty vantage point, Tommy could see Daniels lying on his back and thought he must be dead, until the boy raised his arm slightly. 'Jacko, we have to get over th—'

'Contact,' boomed Adams over the net, and he promptly opened fire on the scrub at the end of the field. This was enough for everybody else to open fire, and the staccato noise hurt their ears as most of the Sergeant's section let rip. Only the two friends opened up from Dashwood's section, as they were the only two that far forward.

'Sergeant Adams, situation report! Over,' screeched Dashwood over the net.

Nothing was heard.

'Sergeant, sit-rep. Over.'

After a second or two, Tommy heard, 'Lance Corporal Jackson, situation report, if you will. NOW.'

Jacko stopped firing his rifle. 'Sir, Private Daniels has been hit. He's down but moving, and the Sergeant's section is laying down suppressing fire on a suspected contact approximately one hundred metres to my front and right. Sir, I suggest me and Tommy try and recover Daniels while the Sergeant's section keeps the contact's head down. Over.'

Lieutenant Richard George Dashwood had dreamed of this situation since he was a small boy. All through his time at Eton and Oxford, he knew he was destined to follow in his father's and grandfather's footprints, to taste and smell the theatre of war and give commands to men who couldn't, to snatch victory from the jaws of defeat, and to be praised for his heroism in saving the day. But at this particular moment in time, it seemed his throat had no moisture in it and his tongue had stuck to the roof of his mouth. He started to feel the awful sensation of his bowels turning to water.

'Sir, did you get my last? Over!' Jacko shouted.

Silence.

'Lieutenant, are you receiving? Over?'

Silence.

'Right, screw this,' Tommy shouted to Jacko. 'Let's go get the poor bastard.'

'Sod it, come on then.' And the two friends jumped up in a cloud of dust and started running across the field towards where Daniels lay.

Lieutenant Dashwood watched with indignation at the two soldiers running across the field. 'What the hell do you think you are doing?' he screamed into his mike. 'Get back in your positions right now, that's an order.'

The two soldiers kept running.

'I don't bloody believe those two reprobates,' he shouted to no one in particular. 'I'll have them on a bloody charge by tonight,' he screamed.

'Permission to help, sir,' shouted Terry from Coventry, and without waiting for an answer, he sprinted after Tommy and Jacko across the field.

'What the…?' stuttered Dashwood, as he watched Terry's large arse disappearing in the dust cloud he was creating. 'Private Smith, get back here, now,' he shouted again into his mike.

What the hell is going on? Dashwood thought. It wasn't supposed to be like this. They were supposed to be following his orders and saving the day and destroying the enemy with British gusto, with him in the lead, as hero.

'Well, it seems to me, sir,' came a voice with an Irish lilt, 'that the radios might not be working too well today…but to be sure the lads have got it all in hand by da looks o' things. I wonder, sir, if it might be best to move up and give them some covering fire?'

'What? Err, oh yes, yes, move up you say, yes, covering fire, yes, that's what we'll do, right. Marvellous.' With that he stood up and, like a World War Two movie star, shouted, 'Right chaps, follow me!' and, swinging his arm up and over his head and pointing forward, moved off across the field.

'What a fuckin' eejit!'

Tommy and Jacko had reached the injured soldier by this time, and they could both see I wasn't good. The bullet had taken him in the side of his face, just below and to the left of his nose, removing part of his cheek bone, the bottom half of his left ear and what looked like part of his skull, although there was so much blood, it was hard to tell. Daniels was still conscious but in shock and was shaking badly. He stared desperately at Tommy as he leaned over him.

'Up ya get, eh, lad,' said Tommy. 'What you doing, lying down on the job then, eh? The Arsehole will have your guts for garters, mate.' Tommy smiled down at the young soldier, concentrating on the terrified eyes so as not to look at the terrible wound. Daniels tried to speak but part of his jaw may have been missing as well, for he could not open his mouth properly and just moaned loudly. When he tried to speak, some of his teeth fell out. Tommy picked these up and put them in Daniels' top pocket. *Well*, thought Tommy darkly, *they can do remarkable things with plastic surgery these days, can't they*.

Jacko moved up beside him and started to retrieve his first aid kit from his belt.

'Jeeeeze,' he said under his breath as he beheld the injury.

'Right, me old mate, I'm gonna have to wrap your face up a bit, ok? I'll try not to hurt you but just shout out if you need to, all right?'

Daniels nodded slightly, so Jacko went to work on bandaging his face. A few moments later Daniels gave an almighty moan, which was probably meant as a scream but was the best he could manage.

'Fuck it,' said Jacko. He reached into his webbing belt and pulled out a morphine syrette and stuck it in Daniels' thigh. After a minute or so his moaning subsided. 'Thank Christ for that. That's gotta to hurt.'

The Sergeant's section was laying on short bursts at the suspected target, with the other section joining in a short time later. Terry skidded to a halt next to Tommy.

'Fuck it, boys, this is no place to be. What's the situation with the lad there?'

Tommy quietly and quickly briefed him on the extent of Daniels' wound.

'Shite,' he said, more to himself that any other. 'Right then,' he keyed his mike, 'Lieutenant, are you receiving? Over.'

'Go ahead. Over.'

'Sir, one casualty with serious wound to head, possibly life threatening. I suggest radio in for immediate heli evac. Over.'

Silence.

'Why did we have to get lumbered with this dickhead?' grumbled Terry.

The radio crackled then. 'Received. Call being made now. What is the situation with contact? Over.'

'Unknown at this time,' Terry replied. 'Suppressing fire seems to be doing the job but suggest two more able bodies with bivvy to remove casualty to a safe area. Over.'

'Standby.'

Silence.

'What a DICK!'

As Terry talked to Dashwood (and himself), Jacko bandaged Daniels' face while Tommy took up a defensive position between his friends and the contact point. He was lying on his stomach, checking the area with his scope. There was nothing to be seen and the contact could either already be dead or had bugged out, but he kept his rifle pointing the right way just in case.

'Right, here we go, transport,' said Terry. 'How close are you, Jacko?'

'Ok, I'm done, and we best be quick. He's just passed out and his breathing is proper shallow.'

Two lads from Adams's section skidded to a halt and unpacked a bivvy. Used as a bivouac normally, today it would be used to stretcher Daniels to a safe area for evacuation.

'Is he good to go, mate?' said one of the soldiers, breathless.

'Yeah, let's get him on,' said Terry, and they very carefully lifted Daniels onto the bivvy. Jacko, Terry and the two others each took a corner and raised him, and prepared to move out. Just at that moment, Tommy shouted out.

'Contact from the front,' and opened fire in short controlled bursts.

'Get moving, Jacko, now!' screamed Tommy, as multiple contacts engaged the platoon from different positions.

'You had better be right behind me, Tommy,' shouted Jacko over his shoulder.

'I'm right on your arse, now fuck off!'

With the wounded soldier being moved quickly out of danger, Lieutenant Dashwood ordered the platoon to make a controlled withdrawal back towards the village whilst he called in for air support and gave the coordinates of the hostile contacts in a somewhat panicky voice. Tommy had heard the instruction from Dashwood while he watched the lads carrying the stretcher, running as best they could whilst trying to keep their heads down. After they had gone about twenty yards or so, Tommy decided he had better make a run for it. With support from both sections of the platoon now laying down covering fire, he jumped up like a jack in the box and made like a whippet after the stretcher bearers, trying to zig zag on the way to make himself less of a target. He could hear Adams bellowing at his section for someone to open up on the bastards with the Gimpy, and a short while later came the heavy rattle sound of the general purpose machine gun as it joined in the staccato noise of the fight.

About bloody time, thought Tommy.

The stretcher bearers were slowing down, which was not surprising, really, since they were carrying dead weight, but they sped up a little when Tommy shouted breathlessly from behind, 'Get a fucking move on, you twats!'

Just as he got within a few yards of the stretcher, the dust around the lads started to kick up like little explosions, and Tommy realised the enemy had a bead on them. Without a second thought, he skidded to a halt, turned and dropped to one knee. Looking through his scope, he attempted to track where the enemy fire was coming from. Within moments he had the image of a black-garbed, heavy, bearded figure firing what looked like an AK47 at his friends. Without hesitation, he opened fire on the figure and immediately saw that his shots were on target. The figure that had once looked like a man was turned into a great, black flying thing as it disappeared arse over tit. Brown hairy mannequin legs, wearing white Nike trainers by the look of it, followed behind. Tommy could have sworn, while later recounting the tale, that he saw meat and two veg as well. It's unbelievable what the brain remembers even in the middle of a firefight.

'Have that, you fucking bastard!' shouted Tommy gleefully. 'Woohoooooo.'

'Tommy!'

He thought he heard someone shouting his name as he continued to scan the edge of the field. Bam! Another target.

'Right, you fucker,' he said to the beardless skinny teenager trying to reload an old rifle. *That was the gun*, he thought, *that took Daniels's face.*

Crack, Crack, Crack.

His SA80 rifle spat at the target. Again, he did not miss, and with the shocking realisation that he was enjoying this, he saw the head of the youth disappear in an explosion of blood, bone and grey matter. Tommy moved a few paces forward, desperate to get another target and avenge young Daniels.

He could hear the rattle of the heavy machine gun, spitting death in a wide arc towards the contact, the *Crack*, *Crack* sound of the combined SA80 rifles of his comrades, and Adams bellowing commands as the platoon drew back to a safer area. Tommy finally understood why he had wanted to be a soldier, and this was it. The adrenalin-pumping, hard-on–giving, mind-boggling simplicity of taking the life of an enemy. This was better than sex, better than anything he had experienced before. He was a god!

'RPG,' someone screamed from the Sergeant's section.

THUMP.

The ground about twenty feet away erupted in a fountain of gravel, sand and shit, spattering all over Tommy. He blinked the dust away and, still on one knee, searched for the culprit who had just fired at him.

You're a shit shot mate, he said to himself. *Ahoy there, my little bearded beauty. And where do you think you're going, hey?* He spotted the figure that had fired the RPG running away, carrying the now-expended weapon. He felt confident enough to take a head shot, but just as he was about to fire the figure turned its head to look back, and he realised it was a woman.

'Oh well, when in Rome,' he muttered.

CRACK.

'Tommy, you fucking idiot,' screamed Jacko. 'Move your arse.'

He turned and realised that in the time it took to dispatch three human beings, the rest of the section had reached cover and safety. Now his radio was starting to get through the fog of battle, and he heard the last bit of a transmission from Dashwood.

'Stop being the fucking hero and get your arse back here, pronto!'

With reluctance, he turned and started to make his way back to the rest of the section. He was still zig zagging and dropping to check for targets. This was the first time he had engaged the enemy properly, and he found that it wasn't so hard. It would be a while before he would be able to describe in clear detail every part of the boy's face that he had killed, or the woman, who would invade his dreams, looking over her shoulder and smiling.

'RPG,' shouted Terry.

Tommy looked over his left shoulder as he ran as an object moved extremely fast in his direction.

'Well bugger me,' was the only thing he could think of, and he threw himself forward towards the ground.

BOOM.

He didn't so much hear the explosion. He felt it.

It was like the time he fell off the top board at the swimming baths, trying to show off for the girls, and he had the sensation of flying in slow motion. The world became a Monet painting, an impression; he couldn't focus on anything while he was spinning through the air.

With a thump, bounced off his head and landed on his back, and he found he couldn't breathe properly. It was as though somebody was sitting on his chest. It had gone strangely quiet and he couldn't hear any gunshots; he couldn't hear anything, actually. Not voices, not birdsong nothing. He was staring up at a clear blue sky and he realised he was going to die.

Bugger! This is going to be hard on Mum and Dad, he thought, *and little Amy, even if she is a teenage bitch*. He could see it now, the coffin draped in the Union flag as it's carried off a Hercules transport, a big procession down the main street in town, flags flying, the regimental colours at the head. There would be people everywhere, crying and throwing flowers on the big black cars; Mum crying and blaming Dad for encouraging him to join the Army. 'You'll have a terrific time, boy,' he had said at the time. He'd be crying as well, and blaming himself too, most likely.

Is the sky lower? Amy might be there too, maybe with that pierced fucking layabout she called a boyfriend, and probably only there because they wanted to get on TV. *Thought it was summer, but it's freezing.* He would miss Pippin though. Great dog but a little yappy sometimes. When Tommy really thought about it, he actually couldn't give two shits for the colours. In fact, he didn't want to be here at all, bleeding out in some Third World shithole.

What's with the fog? Tommy couldn't keep his eyes open any longer, and they felt as heavy as lead. *Perhaps a little nap's in order; it's been a long day.* He turned his head to the side, and just as his vision was darkening he saw the old man from the village, squatting on his haunches at the side of the field, smiling and nodding at Tommy. *Well, at least someone's happy*, he thought, and he closed his eyes.

Chapter 3
Senses

Pain.

Butt-clenching, teeth-grinding, stabbing bloody pain. He could not remember a hangover ever being this shit. Except that New Year's party when he was fifteen and had vomited in the back of his uncle's car – and that was after telling his wife she had a perfect pair of tits.

Hang on though, if I'm in pain, then I'm alive. Isn't that what they say in the movies? 'Pain's good for ya, boy, it lets you know you're alive.' Typical bloody Yank, I bet he never felt this crap. Hang on, if I am alive and the pain is this lousy then…oh shit! Perhaps I've lost part of my head! That's what the pain is! Shit, how the hell will I get a shag with half a head? Mind you, Kerry down the lion will shag anything after a vodka 'n' coke. She did Davey Bull and he's only got one bollock!'

And what's with all the bloody noise then? Loud bloody noises, too. Piss off, will you, and let me wallow in self-pity with half a head. Inconsiderate shits, all of you. I'm a hero, don't ya know. Saved me pals, I did, from an army of ragheads. With machine guns and mortars and tanks! And I think there were enemy planes, too. But I held them off, I did, on my own, wearing a bandana and firing a .50 cal from the hip! Alright, that was old Sly, not me. But I was just as brave as him and better looking, even with half a head.

And what the hell is that smell? Is it Bonfire Night? Used to love Bonfire Night when I was a kid, making mountains out of everybody's crap. Penny for the guy (or we shove dog shit through yer letter box and make life hell for your cat). Fireworks! Rockets, Catherine wheels, star bursts and other shite that cost a fortune, and then just fizzled out in your back garden. Dad always brought some home after work and Mum would make the jacket spuds, and sometimes if we were lucky, sausages. Talking of bangers, now they *were fireworks. Can't get them anymore though, can you? Not surprising though, as they were just grenades for kids. I remember I put a lit one in my cousin's trouser pocket once, a dodgy thing my mate's elder brother got from France, and it nearly blew his knob off! I fell over, I was laughing so hard. Reckon that was a banger them ragheads threw at me, knocked me right on my arse, it did! Bet my cousin's laughing now, twat that he is.*

Urrgghh, what the hell is that under my hand? Oh no, I think I've shit myself. How can a bloody hero with half a head who saved all his mates shit himself? Heroes don't shit themselves, do they? I mean, they haven't gotten any shit to shit, have they! They're shitless ain't they? Sort of. I can smell shit too, real smelly shit. It can't be mine, can it? I mean, I shit roses don't I, being a hero and all that. Perhaps half a head isn't the only injury I got from that raghead's banger! Perhaps half my guts are hanging out; perhaps my intestines are splayed out all around me like a big bloody, pink, shit-smelling octopus. This ain't good, this ain't good at all! Best have a feel and see what's what. Mm… well my head's in one piece by the feel of it. Shame, I was starting to look forward to getting around the back of the Lion and showing Kerry my half a head! Wish this banging would stop though. I don't dare open me eyes. What is that fucking noise? Eh, up, my stomach's still there; no octopus. But what the hell is wrong with my uniform? Why is it so bloody itchy? And it feels like bloody cardboard. Dried blood? Dried shit, maybe? And has someone stolen my webbing? Robbing bloody ragheads, I'm not dead yet, you know. Right, that's it, I'm gonna open my eyes. Right now. Anytime now. Come on, hero, there's nothing to be scared of now, is there? Hero, me, anytime now.

'Jesus Christ, why the hell is it so bright? Arghh, that really fucking hurts,' mumbled Tommy. He closed his eyes quickly and turned his head away from the light. 'Ohhh, that's better. There's that smell again, extremely strong shite.' Tommy opened one eye. 'Hang on, what's that thing?' He squinted. 'It looks like…like…like a horse's arsehole.'

'Jeez,' he shouted and tried to move his head away too quickly. 'Shiiiit,' he moaned as a bomb went off in his skull.

After a few minutes, and with considerable care, he turned back around and indeed found himself to be staring right into the arse of a horse, more than that, a horse that had shit itself.

He started to retch, which made the pain in his head even more acute. *Strange*, he thought, *I don't remember there being any horses around when that banger went off.* Banger! What was he on about, it was a bloody RPG. *And where is that fucking noise coming from?*

'Arghh,' he moaned out loud. He felt like crap and his head was fuzzy, but he was pretty sure there had been no horses in that field when he got hit. He wondered where everybody was and what all the noise was about, so he lifted his head up to look around. Splat! He turned his head to the side and vomited; it landed on the horse's arse, which made him vomit again. With his eyes watering and after a few moments of trying to breathe through his nose and control the nausea, he decided to call for help.

'Jacko.'

Nothing.

'Terry.'

Nothing. Just lots of noise, like people screaming and shout—

BOOM!

Tommy felt a shudder go through him. 'What the hell!' he shouted out loud. He thought another RPG had been fired at him.

Explosions, again and again. Crash! Boom!

Bloody hell, this must be a full on attack by the Taliban, he thought. He rolled over onto his front and put his arms over his head. Bang! This time it was inside his head, and he started retching again.

BOOM!

'Jesus Christ,' he screamed. 'What the fuck is going on?'

He decided to risk a squint and tried to take a careful look around. Concentrating on the terrible pain in his head and trying not to retch again, he looked around slowly from side to side.

He couldn't for the life of him understand why there was fog everywhere. Or was it smoke? His brain was still not functioning properly. *Is somebody using fireworks? There's that smell again*. Slowly, the noises all around became more and more distinct. *Is that a horse whinnying? Surely not!* A man was shouting commands that Tommy didn't understand.

'FIRE.'

'Reload.'

'Go on, ya bloody useless sowars, get after 'em.'

The sound of horses galloping; it was like being at the races.

Voices, strange disembodied voices he didn't know, came drifting out of the fog, smoke or whatever it was; some shouting, some screaming and some even laughing!

'Steady lads, steady.'

BOOM! Another explosion reverberated through the ground under him.

'Private Thompson! If you do not reload that rifle now, you 'orrible little man, I will personally see you on shithouse duty for the rest of your miserable career. Do I make myself CLEAR?'

'Yes Sergeant, sorry Sergeant.'

'You sorry bloody excuse for a soldier.'

'Sorry Sergeant.'

'Stop bloody apologising and load that weapon.'

'Yes Sergeant, sorr–'

BOOM!

Is that gunfire? It doesn't sound like proper rifle fire, Tommy thought. *Ok, ok, I don't know what's going on, but something's not right. Ok, all right, evaluate. I was in the field. Yes! I was running back towards Jacko…*

BOOM!

This latest explosion covered him in a shower of dirt and grit.

'Shit.' Tommy dropped and covered his head again. Pain shot through his eyes, ricocheted around his skull a few times and emptied his stomach of what little contents were left.

'Ooohhhh…crap,' he mumbled, and wiped his mouth. *Perhaps I should just have a quick nap and then I'll be OK*, he thought, and laid his face in the dust and vomit.

Before Tommy's brain could totally give up and close down, a screaming voice, getting closer by the second, was pulling him back from the lovely, fuzzy darkness that was about to envelope him.

That's Pashto, he thought.

He rolled onto his side and managed to look up with one eye closed. For some reason this helped with the pain, and to his mild amusement he saw a large, black-bearded man standing over him, dressed rather garishly in a long white coat, orange leggings and turban. His arm was raised above his head and in his hand was a magnificent curved sword, the sun shining off the blade.

That's really pretty,' thought Tommy for a fleeting moment. The bearded man's black eyes were staring into Tommy's with a look of total confusion, and his mouth was in a rictus of pain or ecstasy, Tommy couldn't tell which. He did notice, though, that the guy had seriously bad teeth and some were black with rot. *Blimey*, he thought, *I bet his breath stinks!*

'What's up with you, then?' he managed to say. 'Why you waving that thing around?'

Then he noticed the red stain spreading across the bearded guy's stomach. And in the middle of this, a shiny pointy piece of metal attached to a wooden branch with a couple of hands holding it. *That's weird looking*, he thought. *Why would that thing be sticking out of his belly?*

With slow motion and a wet sucking sound, the weird branch with the shiny metal thing, which was now red at the end, slid out of the bearded man's stomach. He looked down at his belly and then looked at Tommy, who just shrugged in reply. The man with the turban then proceeded to do an impression of a felled tree.

'PFWEEERHHHHHHHF,' exclaimed Tommy, as the body landed across him.

With the wind firmly knocked out of him and the man lying across him, Tommy thought, *Fuck it!*, and with that, he blacked out.

Pain, butt–clenching – well, pain anyway. But this time there was the added bonus of flying; well, perhaps not flying, more like bouncing. That's it, bouncing, like being on a large space hopper, but lying on your back. *Why would I be lying on my back and bouncing up and down?* thought Tommy. He opened his eyes to find out. Darkness! Not total darkness; there were little lights. Stars! Ah, the night sky. *And it's still bloody hot!* He could feel the sweat trickling down the side of his face. The pain in his head was still there, throbbing in the background. He risked a look sideways and saw – planks. Wooden planks.

'Oh, Christ,' he said, 'I'm dead and this is a coffin.' He looked to the other side: more planks. *Shit, shit, they're lowering me into the ground*, he thought. *In the desert!*

'NO,' he shouted. 'I wanna go home.' He bounced again. 'Ah, no, stop, please,' he shouted. 'Mum and Dad won't be happy. I need to be in St Mary's Church, not in the desert.'

'Easy there, lad.'

'Don't bury me, please.'

'He he, no one's burying anybody lad. Now just lay still there and the Surgeon Major will have you up and about in no time.'

Surgeon?

'Jesus! What's the bloody matter with me?'

'Eh, up there now, there's no need to take the Lord's name in vain.'

Tommy tried to raise his head but failed. He felt weak, and the pain came again behind his eyes and then the sick feeling. He relaxed for a few moments with his eyes closed until it eased off.

Bloody hell, why is it so bumpy? he thought. 'Are we in one of the coffins, mate?' he said to the strange voice.

'Have I not already told ye, yer not getting buried and yer not in a coffin.'

'What! What the hell are you on about? Are we in one of the Rovers or what? 'Cos if we are, the rear shocks need looking at.'

'Well dearie me,' said the voice, 'taken a real thump to yer thought box, haven't ye, young'n. Well, like I already said, the Surgeon Major will see to yer mending.'

Oh for God's sake, thought Tommy, *this guy sounds like a farmer. And who the bloody hell is he? An army medic?*

'Alright mate, listen. What's happened to me, where's my platoon, did the kid make it and what is your bloody name?'

'Calm down, lad,' said the voice. 'The answer to yer last question is Mark, Private Mark Watson. Pleased to make yer acquaintance. And as for yer self, well, yer were knocked for six when that cannon shell landed next to ye and that 'oss of artillery, and you've taken a wound to yer head which I might say won't heal proper if ye keep yelling like yer have been.'

The voice took a deep breath and continued, 'And as for those other questions, well, I don't rightly know, but maybe if ye was to calm down a little, I might go and ask Hospital Sergeant Warren if he knows anything. How does that sound, now, eh?'

Tommy was fully awake now and totally confused. *What did he mean, Hospital Sergeant? And what was that 'oss? Horse of artillery? Horse! Was there a parade or something? He did mean horse, didn't he?'* thought Tommy, *because I have actually seen a dead one out there. Well, a horse's arse anyway.*

He looked over to where he thought the voice might be coming from to see if he could see the man who was talking to him. He could only see the silhouette of his head and shoulders against the dark sky; he couldn't see the bottom half of him at all – but what he could make out did not compute. The man's helmet, if that's what you call it, was not the helmet he was used to, or, for that matter, the helmet used by the British Army. It looked like a big tit!

Not surprisingly, Tommy started to feel a little uncomfortable, and just a little scared.

'Err, listen, mate, could you tell me where I am, please?'

'My name is Mark, lad. Why do ye keep saying mate? Was yer with the navy afore ye joined the regiment?'

What the hell is this guy on about? thought Tommy. *He is properly taking the piss.*

'Listen, mate, I've been shot at, had an RPG lobbed at me, had my head up a horse's arse, been blown up and one of my mates might be dead. So I would appreciate it if you would stop taking the piss and tell me where the hell I am.' Tommy took a deep breath as another wave of nausea hit him. 'Believe me when I say that, if I have to get off this Rover or flat bed or whatever the hell it is, I am seriously gonna kick your arse!'

'Now that will be enough of them profanities. I don't care for that sort of gutter language, do ye hear? If it carries on I will have to report it, understand?'

'Oh, whatever,' Tommy said, exasperated. 'Just take me back to my platoon, will ya?'

'Why are ye so angry, lad? I know yer hurting, but try and be calm or ye will do yer self ill.' Suddenly Tommy heard a sound like a match lighting and turned his head just as a flame lit up the man's face.

'Oh my God,' he said out loud. The flame died as it was sucked into the end of a large pipe, but the image imprinted on his brain was of a face approximately thirty to forty years of age, wrinkled and tanned skin, and a very large moustache. What was also highly strange was the uniform. This guy looked like he had just stepped out of the film *Zulu*. Apart from the fact that his tunic wasn't red but a dirty beige colour, and he came complete with a pith helmet.

Ah! The tit, he thought. *OK, I've had a knock on the head and the rest of the lads are having a laugh, and got this joker with the fake tash to wind me up. That's what it is, panic over. All right, it's pretty realistic, but what else could it be? Right, I will play along and see where it's going.*

'Very well, Mark, I apologise for the profanities. It's just that I'm feeling a little out of sorts this evening.' He had to smile at his attempt at being posh. 'I would be terribly grateful if you could tell me where we are headed and why?'

'Oh, well then, that's more like it, lad, much better. Well, it was like this, see, ye was found union – unconsha – asleep. Next to a dead 'oss of artillery. And lying across yer was one of them backstabbing levies who had been stuck by one of our boys straight through his backstabbing gizzard.' He took a breath. 'Well, after that little scrap, me and some of the other lads went poking round looking to see if any of our lot was lying injured or what not, and that's when we found ye, lad.'

Tommy had to give this guy credit. He was doing a fantastic job of playing a character from that *Zulu* movie. *And any time now*, he thought, *he will start singing 'Men of Harlech' in a dodgy Welsh accent.*

'Thank you for saving me, Mark.' *This is getting good.* 'Would you mind telling me our destination, please?'

'Well, lad, according to Major Preston, we will be heading for a village. I can't recall the name of it, couldn't prun, prunon, say it! Even if I knew, anyways, well, it's about half way back towards Kandahairy.'

'Kandahar.'

'That's what I said.'

Tommy sighed heavily.

'So, Mark, what did the levies do that was so terrible, then?'

'Well, lad, seeing that ye don't remember, those backstabbers was supposed to be on our side and they ended up turning their coats, ya see. But the old General, well, he won't have any of that, will he, so he has the Cavalry pretty boys take a run at 'em, them heathen. Ghazis, most likely, and they were no match for our galloping gunners or the 66th, and we took their guns off 'em.'

This guy is quite adept, thought Tommy. *He knows his stuff.* And Tommy knew that Mark knew his stuff because he'd gotten a B+ in his A-level history exam at school. He had always had an interest in the military, right from an early age, and he recalled the army language that was used in the days of tribesmen, cavalry and levies. If memory served him, the 'Ghazi' were religious fanatics during the Afghan wars. He thought harder as he bumped and bounced along to God knows where. Galloping gunners he was sure was an artillery unit, but the

66th he wasn't so sure about. Infantry maybe? He continued to play along with the joke.

'Mark, me old mate, who are the 66th?'

'Have ye lost yer memory altogether, then, lad? 'Tis yer own regiment, of course.'

'Sorry, Mark, but will you humour me? I think that bang on the head was a lot harder than I thought.' *Let's see if this trips him up*, he thought.

'The 66th Regiment of Foot, lad, ye know? The Berkshires. Ye making fun of me now?'

Ah, thought Tommy, *now it's starting to come together. The Berkshires! The 66th! Of course, they were famous for…famous for… oh crap, famous for what? Think, think. Got it! They were involved in a battle in the 1800s somewhere near Kabul. Ah ha!* he thought, *got him. We're nowhere near Kabul. So this this fella doesn't know his history. Right then.*

'So, when are going to get to Kabul, then Mark? Because at this rate, it's gonna be next year.'

'I already said, lad, we're going somewhere near Kandahairy. Have yer ears stopped working as well? Do ye smoke, lad? I've some excellent shag here.' Mark continued to puff away at his pipe, looking at the stars as if without a care in the world.

Bump!

'Ouch,' said Tommy, as his head bounced off the planking to the side of him. 'Right, that's it,' and with that, he pushed himself up onto his elbows to look at what he was riding in. He could just see over the rim of the cart. Cart! *Why the hell have they got me in a cart?* he thought, and, *Oh no, not that again!* He flopped down onto his back again. Another horse's arse, albeit a live one and not covered in shit!

'Oh, stop with the game now, Mark, or whoever you are. It's getting boring and I'm tired and I've got a splitting headache. Just take us back to base, would you?'

'Well, why don't ye close yer eyes, lad, and get some rest. We have a way to go yet.'

Tommy closed his eyes. He was, after all, far too tired to continue the game. *What the hell?* he thought. *You win.* And fell asleep.

With a bemused look Mark Watson, private and medic, puffed on his pipe again. Finding that it had gone out, he reached into his pocket but could not find his matches. 'Jesse, Jesse, lad, would you have a match on you?'

Standing on the other side of the horse and cart, Private Jesse Holmes, medic, nodded and reached for his matches, 'Ay, Mark, I do,' and threw them to his comrade. 'Do ye think he's lost his mind, this one?' Nodding towards Tommy.

Mark shook his head. 'I don't know, Jesse, lad, but he don't sound right, do he? I think mayhap the Surgeon Major can fix him up.'

'He talks funny, though, and he kept saying strange things.' Jesse shook his head slowly. 'Reckon he's from London town, you think, with all those fancy words he has?'

'I don't rightly know, lad, but hush ye now, we have a long way to go and this boy needs to sleep.'

The horse and cart, with Tommy lying unconscious in the back, and with Privates Watson and Holmes escorting it, followed the baggage train of the 66th Berkshire Regiment, and trundled off into the night, and into history.

Chapter 4
Dream

*T*he nipples are too large and way too dark. Mind you, this bird is a darky anyway, so they're supposed to look like that, ain't they? She is properly gorgeous: fantastic body, tall, slim in the waist, although her arms are way too hairy and she should get her moustache trimmed.

The biker look is way behind the times, love, he thought. She dunked her head in the barrel again and came up spraying water in a lovely large rainbow of colours. *She has unusually long hair, this one. Really long, nearly all the way down to her… Oh! Now that is kinky! She's wearing boots. Riding boots at that, or biker boots in her case, and jodhpurs by the look of 'em. Oh, to have them wrapped round my back! Hang on, what is she doing now? She's stretching or something, aerobics maybe. Oh, look at that. She can bend all the way down without bending her knees. Sexy! What is she throwing her arms round for? Kung fu! She knows kung fu as well! Just look at those moves she's making. She's well hard. Hard and sexy. Well, maybe not the moustache or the hairy arms, but everything else? Gorgeous! I wonder if she would be interested in a drink in the Lion or something. Or a movie, or we could just take a walk along the river; I don't live far from here. Think I'll ask her…*

'Hooch.' *God my mouth's dry*. Tommy coughed. 'Ah that's better. Hello, how are you then, gorgeous?'

Is that my voice? I sound like Frank Bruno or something. Eh, up then, here we go. She's looking over. Be calm, son, you can do this. Ah, don't put your top back on. Well, actually, maybe you can because you've got no tits and that tuft of hair in the middle of your chest is nasty. But that don't matter, don't matter at all. I've had

38

worse down Bogeys on an '80s night, and they were fat as well as ugly. She's coming over, shit, she's coming towards me. Why is she putting her hair in a bun, or whatever you call it? Strange, but sexy in a grandmotherly sort of way. Look at the length of those legs, she must be six foot. She's coming over, right into my bedroom and straight through the wall, how funky is that? Mind you, my dad won't be happy; he'll have to repaper again. Can you still get Power Ranger wall paper? She's leaning over me. Well I'm gonna get a snog here. Wow! What lovely blue eyes. Eh, eh, hang on, where are you going? And there's no need to shout. Is that Spanish or something? Yeah, oh yeah, she's a sexy Spanish biker chick! Who's that? Oh crap! Is that my old man? It is, damn it, and he's talking to the biker chick and pointing. Shit! Dad's coming over, he's leaning over and putting a hand on my forehead.

'I don't wanna go to school today, Dad. I feel sick.'

The biker chick is saying something to him. Is she trying to chat up my dad? Slapper!

'He's married, you know, to my mum, and he's too old for ya.'

'Easy now, go back to sleep, there's a good lad.'

'Sorry Dad. OK, I am a bit tired. I got blown up today, yesterday, sssomething. I got, got…'

Darkness.

I love camping. Camp fires, a bit of weed, some beer and shagging. Camping's brilliant! It reminds me of when me and Dad used to go all the time at weekends. Mind you, I didn't shag or smoke or drink then, not with my dad. That was when I was a teenager, with my mates. Oh no, me and Dad used to make fires and tell ghost stories and eat fried food, like bacon and eggs. Some of my mates used to take the piss, saying he was old fashioned and stuff. Well, he was old; he didn't have me till quite late in life. But he's still cool! He would tell me stories about his time in the national service, and about the places he was posted. He would tell me about the things he got up to in West Germany. That's why I wanted to join the army in the first place, to fight for my country; defender of the faith and all that. Not actually like that though, is it, in reality? I mean, in reality it can be blood, guts, pain, fear and shitting yourself. Yeah, reality is a funny thing sometimes. Anyway, camping! Yep, I love camping, always have. Sometimes though, it can be bloody uncomfortable. Like now. This camp bed is proper lumpy. And why is it when I open my eyes, it looks like I'm under water? Talking of water, my mouth feels as dry as a Pharaoh's sock!

'Hello,' Tommy croaked. 'Hello, is anybody there?'

No answer.

Tommy was lying on his back. He opened his eyes again. *Oh wow!* he thought, *I feel stoned.* He tried to focus his gaze straight up, and he could just make out what looked like a khaki-coloured roof. After a few more moments of blinking, he realised it was a tent roof; he could also see the cross pole. Trying to recall how he came to be staring at the khaki-coloured roof of a tent, he suddenly remembered that he had been hit by a banger – idiot! It was an RPG. *Right then*, he thought, *I must be injured. Yes, that's it. I've taken an injury and that's why I'm here. This is a hospital tent, then. But I can't be that bad because the lads were taking the piss, weren't they? You know, bringing me in on a cart instead of a heli. Ha! Very bloody funny, that.*

'Oi, can anybody bloody hear me?' Tommy said, louder this time. 'I'm gonna die of thirst here, you know.'

'I can hear you,' said a deep voice. 'I will get you some water in good time, so please keep your voice down. There are some sick individuals in here, thank you.'

Ah! Tommy thought, *I'm not alone, then.* He moved his head, following the voice, but he still could not focus properly. His head felt like lead when he tried to move it. He could just make out a blurred figure sitting at a desk with what looked like a candle burning on it, and Tommy could not help but smile at this.

'Bloody typical,' he said to the figure. 'They can't even be bothered to pay the electric bill, let alone supply us with decent kit.' Tommy sighed. 'Wankers!'

'Now listen here, Private,' said the blurred figure. 'Please keep your voice down and your comments to yourself, there's a good chap. I will be with you in but a moment.'

Well lardy fucking da.

Tommy tried to focus on his surroundings, moving his eyes slowly around the room – tent. It was obviously a tent, he could see that now, even with the blurred vision. The thought of camping with his father came back to him and he had to swallow down an involuntary sob. He took a deep breath and continued to scan around. There were other beds in here as well, three he could count, two of them occupied. Why hadn't they flown him out yet? And better still, why wasn't he in a proper hospital in Kandybar? This thought confused him; in fact, everything confused him: The cart he had been on with the horses, the bogus soldier with the dodgy hat and fake moustache, some raghead with a bloody marvellous curved sword…Was that real?

Was any of it real? What about that girl, with the long hair and kinky boots? Where was she, and was she a nurse perhaps? When he thought about it, she was a right dog, actually, with all that facial hair. Oh well, any port in a storm, especially a port with such long legs. He looked around the tent and was shocked to see how basic it was. *Oh brilliant. I'm in a Red Cross camp! How fantastic!* he thought. *Blown up, nearly carved up and dragged around on a sodding horse and cart, and now the local witch doctor at a Red Cross camp.*

Tommy sighed loudly. 'Any time today, Doc,' he said.

Suddenly the girl appeared at his bed side with a clay jug and cup. *Christ!* thought Tommy. Even with the blurred vision, he could see she was a moose.

'You would like a drink of water, Private Sahib?'

What the bloody hell is wrong with her voice?

'Just a little, if you please, Arun. I would like to check our erudite young Private before he starts to guzzle too much of that.'

Tommy followed the voice and turned to find the blurred figure standing and walking towards him. With his vision starting to clear, he could now see the doctor; he presumed the man was a doctor, about 5'10" and maybe about thirty, thirty-five years old. He stopped at the side of the bed and leaned over.

'Well, Private, how are we feeling, eh?'

'How do you think I'm bloody feeling? I feel crap, mate. And can you tell me why I'm not in a hospital, 'cause I think I should be in one. And where are the lads I was with? One of them was injured, shot in the face.'

While he was talking, the doctor was checking him over, first his temperature with a hand on the forehead, then a lift of his eye lids, one at a time, staring into them. 'All in good time, Private, all in good time,' came the reply. 'Now then, how does the head feel? Any pain, blurred vision, stars in front of your eyes?'

Oh, for Christ's sake, thought Tommy. *Typical bloody uni grad getting his kicks in a war zone so he can bore his future bloody GP patients to death with his war stories. OK, OK, that's OK, let's do as he says.*

'Well Doc-tor,' said Tommy, in his best Marylyn Monroe voice, 'my eyes are just starting to clear and the only pain I have now is in my ass!' With that he gave him a big toothy smile.

'I think that will be quite enough of that, Private. I asked you a civil question so kindly answer me. Oh, and do try not to forget my rank this time.'

Rank! Shit, he's army. Injuries or not, rank's rank!

'Sorry, sir. I'm not feeling too bright and my head feels real fuzzy, and I'm not thinking straight. In fact, I could have sworn I was at home and my dad was here. I called out to him when I thought he was talking to your nurse there.' He nodded to the other side of the bed.

The doctor looked confused for a second, and then tried to hide his smile behind a cough. He looked over to the girl with the long legs, smiled and said, 'Well, Arun, what say you, woman? Did you talk to this young man's father?'

'No, I – No, Major Preston Sahib, there was no one else here.' The confused look on Arun's face made the doctor chuckle.

Tommy just stared at Arun, quite unable to place what he found so unusual about her, until, with a realisation that made him exclaim out loud, he realised Arun the nurse was, in fact, a man! With a moustache…and a hairy chest.

Tommy closed his eyes and tried not to think of all the dirty thoughts he'd had about Arun and her, sorry, *his*, long legs. *Oh shiiiit!*

'Now then, Private, the reason you are in my tent is by way of a knock on the head during our little skirmish with the not-so-loyal levies of Mr Shere Ali. You were found next to a dead trooper and his horse, and by the look of it, you have suffered a possible fracture to your skull. To help you sleep and to control the pain, I have been administering laudanum, during your more lucid moments, of course.' He frowned down at Tommy. 'But you have been experiencing some severe hallucinations, so I have decided to cease the use of laudanum for now and see how we go from there. You say there is no pain in the head at the moment, just feeling a little fuzzy? Good, that would only be the effects of the medication. Now then, why don't you accept that drink of water off the lovely Miss Arun here, and I will just finish up on my notes.'

With that, he walked back over to his desk and continued what he was doing.

'Hang on, Doc. Is this a Red Cross station or what?'

'I am afraid, Private, that the Lord Wantage's folly has yet to reach this infernal hell hole.'

Lord Wantage! Did he have something to do with the founding of the Red Cross? Tommy didn't understand a thing about what the doctor – Major – was saying. Could this be a continuation of the lads' big joke? *It's a bit too elaborate, to say the least*, he thought, and the place he was in right now looked far too real. And, he suddenly realised, unless this was the set of a play, the honourable doctor there looked dashing in his, well, he wasn't sure what uniform it was, but it looked convincing. *And if this isn't a joke and I'm not dreaming then…Oh! Oh dear.*

'I'm dead,' Tommy whispered.

'Pardons, Private Sahib.'

Tommy looked up at Arun, who was holding the jug and cup in front of him like some sort of peace offering, and returned his gaze with a rather docile looking smile.

'I'm dead, aren't I?' said Tommy.

Arun stared at Tommy for a few moments.

'If Private Sahib was dead,' he said, looking confused again, 'why is he asking for a drink of water?'

Tommy closed his eyes. 'Oh no, no, no, no this can't be happening.'

'Pardons, Private Sahib, what is can't be happening?'

'This! All this – shit, what is this? If this is death, then is this heaven or hell? Is it that purgatory thingy? What the fuck is going on? Where am I?'

'My apologies, Private Sahib, but I am not understanding. Do you wish me to fetch the Surgeon Major Sahib?'

'Are you some kinda nutcase?' Tommy gaped at Arun, 'How can you be a nutcase in heaven – hell – whatever! Can you just please tell me if this is the afterlife, you know, an afterlife hospital or something? And can I see my granddad, Stan? He should be here somewhere.'

Arun started to back away with a slightly horrified and confused look.

'Where are you going? Can you answer me, please?'

'I, um, I will fetch Surgeon Major Sahib for you, yes, please.'

'What! He's over there,' Tommy turned to find that the doctor was not at the desk, so he turned back to Arun, who had also disappeared.

'This isn't fair,' he shouted to no one. He found himself sitting up in bed – well, it was more like a cot, really, and bloody uncomfortable. 'Bollocks to this.'

He pulled aside the itchy, hairy brown blanket and swung his legs out – which, to his relief, he still had. He placed his feet gingerly on the rough ground, but then had to stop because the tent started to sway.

'Ohhh, crap.'

Right, OK, one step at a time, he said to himself. Tommy stood with shaking legs; he took a hesitant step forward and nearly fell.

'Bollocks,' he said again. He took another step, and another. *All right, that's more like it*, he thought, and stood still, turning slowly as he scanned his surroundings.

The tent was indeed sparse – nothing but four beds, some wooden buckets, a couple of old wooden stools and a desk with a candle on it. He walked carefully over to the desk, but before he got there, he stopped, tilted his head and listened. *Is that horses again?* he thought. And now more sounds. *People, lots of people*, he thought, *talking, shouting and laughing. And different noises; saws at work maybe?* There were hammers banging, a metallic ringing as if a smith was working over an anvil. *Or something like that, anyway.* Why hadn't he heard this before? *The drugs! That must be it. What did the doc say? Laudanum, that was it. Bloody opiates! Great, I'm a smackhead!*

Tommy started to feel woozy again, so he leaned on the desk. Steadying his breathing, he looked across the top of the desk and found a leather-bound diary. Next to this was a polished wooden box with a hinged lid. He reached over and opened the box, which was more like a highly ornate case with brass locks. What he found inside made him properly confused. *Am I in a bloody museum?* he thought. *What's with the antiques?*

Inside were numerous instruments, *Of a medical origin*, he thought. Scissors, scalpels, other peculiar objects and a selection of saws. Small metal saws. He shuddered at the look of them. There were also a few little bottles with attached labels handwritten in pen. He picked one up and read it. *Chloroform.* He could just manage to decipher the handwriting. He read another, this one a large glass jar. *Hemp.* He placed it back in the box, still no clearer on their meaning, or on anything, to be exact. He moved around the desk and opened the diary. It was full of the most beautiful handwriting, sketches and mathematical calculations. He flipped to the last page and started to read.

19 July, 1880. Subject: Male, approx. 20–25 years.
The subject is an unusual one, for I have never encountered such a severe case of psychosis. The young Private (I have yet to confirm his name) is suffering from a complete loss of contact with reality. Given the nature of the wound suffered to the cranium, I would have expected some impairment to insight, but this young

man has invented an entirely new reality for himself. For the past three days, he has continually asked for family members and to be taken to the nearest military hospital, and, in his own words, 'A Yank one will do.' What the colloquialism for the Americas is for, I have no idea. He also insists that he was in a platoon and one of his 'mates' had taken a gunshot wound to the face, but as we have no clear understanding of the identity of this young man or his platoon, he remains anonymous. I have discontinued the use of laudanum, for although he was released from the pain in his head, his hallucinations were becoming extreme.

Addition: On a lighter note, with regards to his delusions, he thought my wallah was a female and actually tried to engage him in courting rhetoric.

Tommy stood stunned for a moment, leaning against the desk. His thoughts were a jumble of shock, incredulity, panic and hilarity, thoughts so fantastic, he wanted to laugh and scream at the same time. If his eyes hadn't deceived him, or maybe it was the opiates, he was in fact in a hospital tent, in lust with a long haired man, and, according to the diary's date, it was 1880. The world spun for a second and Tommy landed on his arse with a thud.

'Ere, you right, boy?' came a voice from one of the other beds.

Tommy looked at the occupant. He found a balding man with a large nose and an awful skin condition. He smiled. 'No, I'm not OK, mate.'

He started to giggle, then laugh, loudly, at the insane position he found himself in.

Well, I suppose it's better than being dead, he thought, *or maybe I am dead and this is my afterlife after all.*

'Hang on a minute,' he said.

'Hang on to what, boy?'

'Well, it can't be death, can it? I mean, I'm still breathing and all that, and I feel pain and all.'

'Have ye lost yer mind, then?'

'Pardon?'

'Is thee mad?' the voice said. 'God's marcy, ye bin booming since ye waayked.'

Tommy laughed again. 'I have no idea what you're talking about, mate, but it sounds great.'

'Take no mind to him,' said a voice from the other bed. 'Miserable bugger, he is.'

Tommy looked to the occupant of the other bed and saw a young man, maybe in his twenties and extremely pale looking.

Tommy grabbed hold of the edge of the desk and pulled himself up; he stood for a moment, not quite knowing what to do.

'Are you all right, old boy? You look rather pale, don't you know.'

Tommy laughed at that. 'You wanna have a look in a mirror, me old mate. You look like Casper.'

The young pale man smiled, but looked confused as well. 'Well, I am sure that Mister Casper is devilishly handsome as well.'

They both laughed at this remark.

'I honestly don't know what to do,' said Tommy. 'I think maybe I'm going mad. I shouldn't be here. I mean, I was somewhere else, and now I'm here, dead or in the past or maybe just stoned…I dunno!'

'Well it certainly appears you had a little bump on the head all right, but a word of advice, my friend: I wouldn't go spouting off too much about being dead or in the past or whatever stoned means. I dare say you will be carted off back to jolly old England and deposited in the nearest asylum.'

Tommy stared at Mr Pale for a few moments, and then said, 'What if this is just a dream? What if I've been injured and I'm in a coma or something? And this is all just a very weird dream.'

'Well I must say, if this is a dream, I feel terribly real, and since I feel terribly real, I will introduce myself. Lieutenant Maurice Rayner, at your service, Adjutant with the 66th Berkshire Regiment. Oh, and I do a spot of interpreting as well, just in case you want to ask the lovely nurse out for dinner, what.'

Tommy had to smile at this. As he walked over to the Lieutenant, he held out his hand and said, 'Thomas Evans, Private, the Queen's Own Fusiliers, nutcase!'

Rayner shook it. 'Well, Private Evans, I don't recall the fusiliers being part of our little party, so unless you are quite mad, or have gotten lost out here in this bloody furnace, I suggest you become a private in the Berkshires, because if the skilled Surgeon Major comes to the conclusion that you are, in fact, insane, then its cheerio to dear old Private Evans, hello asylum!'

Tommy thought about this for a while whilst listening to the hustle and bustle outside the tent. *What the hell*, he thought. *If I'm dead then none of this will matter, and if I'm in a coma, well, there's no point fighting it, just go where it takes me. As for going back in time, well, that's just silly.*

'All right, sir,' said Tommy in a smart voice. 'Private Evans of the 66th reporting for duty. Must beg your pardon, sir, as I seem to have mislaid my memory, and this Private begs your indulgence.'

Chapter 5
Friend

There is a distinct smell to a hospital, a clinical smell, a smell of TCP, disinfectant, Savlon, chemical smells in general. The strange smell here, though, Tommy couldn't place. He had never liked the smell of hospitals; it meant sickness and death. It also meant watching your loved ones take their last breath, like Granddad Stan, curled up on a bed fighting for every breath; six stone soaking wet and looking a hundred-and-fifty-years-old. He didn't always look like that though; no, once he was a big man. A big strong man and a soldier, it's true. Tommy had seen all the old photographs from the war when he was a child. All those black and white prints of young Stan and his mates, standing alongside burnt out German tanks, artillery pieces and even brothels (though he wasn't supposed to see those photos, and Gran went mad when Tommy asked who the black girl was sitting on his lap, drinking out of a champagne bottle).

'Ah, well now,' Stan had said, 'that was a poor Nubian that I rescued from the Nazis, boy. Poor girl was so happy when we took that French town, she gave us all a drink and a kiss, as thanks, you know.' And with that he had quickly buried the photo at the bottom of the shoe box where they were kept.

He was at Dunkirk as well. Three days, he was on that beach. He only ever spoke about that when he'd had a drink, and even then not much; it was the only time during the war when he had been truly frightened. There was one occasion, though, when he'd gotten quite drunk, and it was then that Stan told Tommy a secret.

It was the third day on the beach at dusk and he had just waded back after the Destroyer he had tried to board had taken a direct hit from a Stuka dive bomber. When he got back to the hole he had dug in a sand dune, he found another soldier hiding in it. He had gotten into an argument with the man, who had point blanked refused to move, with Stan arguing that he had dug that hole with his own two hands. Just then, as a fight was about to ensue, a German ME 109 fighter came screaming down the beach heading straight for them. As the other soldier's attention was taken up with the fighter, Stan thumped him in the stomach and dragged him out of the hole and dived in. In between sobs, he said, 'I watched that poor boy disintegrate right in front of me, lad. He was gazing right at me and then he was gone. Why, why did I do it? There was room for the two of us.' Tommy left his Granddad crying, alone in his potting shed, and it was never mentioned again.

'What is it?' Tommy asked, as Arun passed him a wooden bowl with what looked like vomit in it.

'It is food, Private Sahib.'

'Yes, I can see that it might be food, but what sort of food?'

'Err, it is being wholesome food, Private Sahib,' and with that Arun walked back out of the tent.

Tommy sighed heavily and sniffed the contents of the bowl. *Well*, he thought, *it smells like soup or stew or something like that, anyway. How is it that, if this is the afterlife, I'm not eating huge hunks of pork and beef, and bowls filled with all different kinds of fruit, and drinking wine, and getting a bed bath from a group of virgins?* He sighed again and, picking up the wooden spoon, placed a small amount of it in his mouth. With a mighty effort, he started to chew.

It might be a potato stew, he thought after a moment. *And maybe some meat as well.* He stopped chewing, and swallowed quickly. *Meat!* he thought again. *What kind of meat?* He inspected the bowl, stirring the contents up and checking the bit of gristle he had managed to find. *Beef*, he thought, *that's got to be beef, probably the testicles or some other offal.* But he was hungry, very hungry, he realised. In fact, he couldn't remember the last time he had eaten; he thought it might have been a packet of crisps on the morning of the patrol. *Morning! What time is it now? What day is it now? Do they have days here?* Tommy thought. *Am I going mad or something?*

'Sod it,' he said, and threw the rest of the stuff down his throat.

'My, who's a hungry boy, then?' came a voice from the tent flap. 'Don't forget to stop at your fingers, what.'

Tommy looked up and saw Lieutenant Rayner standing by the tent entrance. He smiled and licked the spoon. 'Not too bad actually when you don't think about what's in it.'

'Food of the gods, I'm sure.' The Lieutenant limped over to his bed and climbed onto it. With an exaggerated sigh, he collapsed back onto the roughly stuffed pillow. 'That, my fine fellow,' he said 'was an awful lot of work just to have a shit.' He rolled onto his side and faced Tommy. 'Feel any better, Mr Dead and Gone to Hell?'

Tommy placed the bowl on the little stool next to his bed, swung round and sat on the edge. 'You can take the piss all you want, Maurice, but I know what my eyes are telling me, and they're telling me that, unless I'm dead, I'm asleep and dreaming. If I'm not dreaming, then I'm as mad as a box of frogs, and if I'm not mad, then I've gone back in time, for what reason I couldn't tell ya. Personally, my money's on the dreaming.'

'Well, I don't care for any of those scenarios.' Maurice leaned up on his elbow, 'Because, Thomas, if you are dead, then I'm a ghost, if you are dreaming, then I don't exist, if you are insane, then I am just a figment of your overactive imagination and if you have indeed gone back in time, as you say, then I have already lived this life and I am, well, already dead!' He smiled at Tommy. 'Saying that, though, at least I get to live again. Even in your mind will do.'

Tommy sat thinking for a moment. *What if Maurice is right?* As insane as it sounded to Tommy, what if he had gone back in time? He looked over at Maurice, then looked around the tent, and thought, *How could this be a dream? It's so real!* He had never had a dream like it; in fact, he couldn't recall ever having a dream and realising it was a dream at the same time. *Can you even do that?*

'Why the bloody hell would I have gone back in time? What possible reason would there be for that to happen? No, no, I'm obviously dreaming or something, because, you know what, I can feel pain. How can you feel pain when you're dead? Eh? Tell me that, then, Maurice.'

'You can feel pain, old bean, because you are indeed alive! As we sit here debating on the why's and wherefores of heaven and hell, your heart is pumping blood to that close approximation you call a brain. You are also, I might add, breathing. You have just eaten some of that slop, for goodness sake. And believe me, if you weren't real, I would be the first to tell you.' With that, he leaned down from the bed, picked up a wooden bowl and threw it at Tommy, catching him in the leg.

'Ow! Why did you do that?' exclaimed Tommy. 'That bloody hurt!'

'Aha!' shouted Maurice. 'You can feel pain, you are alive and I am a genius, as I always knew I was.'

'I already told you I could feel pain,' complained Tommy.

'Yes, yes, I was testing your theory, so please don't ruin my moment of triumph.'

Just at that moment, the tent flap parted and the Surgeon Major walked in, followed by another, rather large officer, by the look of him, or so Tommy thought.

'You, young man, are supposed to be resting that head of yours. Now swing those legs back up and lie down, or I will tell the Sergeant Major here that you are fit for duty. I'm sure he could find you plenty of jobs to do.'

'Yes sir, sorry sir,' replied Tommy, and he swung his legs back up onto the bed.

Tommy looked at the Sergeant Major and found him staring back, looking from underneath the bushiest eyebrows he'd ever seen. This was a big man, at least six-foot-five or six, broad in the chest and shoulder, and standing ramrod straight.

He had a large moustache and beard as well, though they were well groomed. In fact, he looked quite magnificent. He was wearing an off-white uniform, all shiny brass buttons and a pith helmet. He gave off an air of absolute confidence, and Tommy felt slightly intimidated.

'Now then, Sergeant Major, you wished to see Corporal Armour. You will find him in that bed over there,' the Surgeon Major said, pointing to the third occupant of the tent. Then he went and sat at his desk.

The man in the other bed had suddenly lost the colour in his face and he was visibly shaking. The Sergeant Major walked over to the foot of the bed and looked down. *This guy is brilliant*, Tommy thought. *He seriously looks the part, and even comes with one of those cane thingies.*

'Now then, Armour, would you like to explain to me why you are not back with your chums and performing your duties like a good soldier? Because the Surgeon Major here has told me your wounds have healed and you are fit for duty.' He paused his slow, sonorous voice for obvious effect. 'Now, for some strange reason you, have told the Surgeon Major that you are not fit for duty, that you have not fully recovered from your wounds and you are refusing to leave the Surgeon Major's tent, a tent for genuinely injured soldiers.' He took an enormous inhalation through his nose while looking above at the roof. 'Now then, sonny, if I were to think that what you were in fact experiencing was not sickness but, say, cowardice, for instance, well, I would have to report it to the General. And I would presume that he would make an example of you to the rest of the regiment. The Cat hasn't seen the sunshine in many a year.' He gave Armour a piercing stare. 'So I will ask you, Corporal Armour, are you or are you not fit and ready for duty?'

The man Armour jumped out of bed and stood at attention, and barked, 'Corporal Armour ready and fit fer duty, Sergeant Major Cuppage.'

The big Sergeant Major nodded like a proud father. 'Well done, lad. Now you have a little time to get your things together, and then report to Sergeant Rollings's Company.'

'Yes Sar'nt Major Cuppage,' Armour nearly shouted.

The big Sergeant Major turned and started to make his way back to the entrance. But he caught site of Maurice and stopped. 'Well, I did not see you there, Lieutenant Rayner. You are making a speedy recovery, I hope, sir?'

'I am, Sergeant Major, thank you. You are well yourself?'

'I am in excellent health, sir.'

'Tell me, Sergeant Major, have you met our new arrival?' he asked, nodding toward Tommy. 'No? Well, may I introduce Private Thomas Evans, formally of the Fusiliers, newly joined in India and now a man of the 66th. Private Evans, may I introduce Sergeant Major Alexander Cuppage, backbone of the regiment.'

For a moment Tommy forgot where he was and put out his hand for Cuppage to shake. The Sergeant Major looked at it with indifference and then looked back at Tommy. He realised his mistake and jumped out of bed and came to attention. 'Pleased to make your acquaintance, Sar'nt Major.'

'Indeed,' he said. 'And what is wrong with you, exactly? For you look healthy and well fed to my eyes.'

'I was caught by an RPG, Sergeant Major,' replied Tommy, without a thought for what he had just said.

Cuppage raised his bushy eyebrows. 'An RPG, you say. Very good. And what, pray tell, is an RPG?'

'I am afraid, Sergeant Major,' intervened Surgeon Major Preston, 'that the young Private has taken a knock to his head, and, well, frankly talks nonsense now and then. But he is recovering, albeit slowly.'

Realising his mistake, Tommy said, 'Sorry, Sar'nt Major, what I meant to say was a cannon. Yes, a cannon shell took me off my feet.' He wanted to laugh but kept a straight face.

'Indeed. Very well, lad, I pray you make a speedy recovery.' He turned to Preston and Rayner, nodding at them in turn, and said, 'Good day, sirs.' Then he made his way to the entrance. But as he got there, he turned and looked at Tommy, who felt that, for some strange reason, the Sergeant Major was seeing right into his mind. After a moment Cuppage shook his head as if to clear it, and then left.

'Well, that was strange,' said Rayner.

'What was?' replied Tommy.

'Well, my erstwhile friend, it seems as if you spooked old Cuppage. I mean, what was that look about, as though he'd seen a ghost or something?' He realised what he'd said, 'Oh damn it all.'

'Ah ha,' exclaimed Tommy. 'There you go, mate, now you're talking.'

'Talking about what?' asked Preston.

'Oh, it's nothing, Major, sir. More ramblings from Private Evans. But there is improvement, wouldn't you say? Every day, yes indeed.'

'Hmm, well that remains to be seen, Lieutenant Rayner. Now if you will excuse me, gentlemen, I have to attend the smoothbore battery.' He made his way to the entrance. 'It seems we may have a case of cholera. If you need anything, please instruct my wallah Arun to attend you.' He nodded and then left the tent.

Tommy was lost in thought until Private Armour dropped something with a loud clang in his haste to pack. Tommy and Maurice looked at each other and started to laugh.

'What ye laughing at, eh? And you should know better, Lieutenant, being a young gentleman and all.'

'You are quite correct, Joseph. It is Joseph, yes? On behalf of Thomas and myself, please accept our apologies for the puerile behaviour.'

'Well that would be, well, alright then, sir.' Armour didn't know what else to say to the two young men, so he just nodded, picked up his kit and left.

'What a tosser,' said Tommy.

'I would agree with you, Thomas, but I have no idea what a tosser might be, so I will assume it means a malingerer of sorts, what.'

'Yep,' replied Tommy.

'Very well, Thomas, we have managed to get our poor injured brother in arms evicted. Now I think it's time we shared a little snifter, what.' He reached down to the floor, picked up what looked like a canvas bag, opened it and produced a green glass bottle with a flourish and held it aloft like a trophy.

'What's that, then, mate?'

'My dear Thomas, this little beauty and I have travelled far and wide, from England to India, and now to our little haven.' Maurice handled the bottle as you would a baby. 'This, Thomas, is an 1865 Hardy cognac that I picked up from London, and I have been saving it to share with a friend. So what say you, Thomas, will you procure a couple of crystal glasses so we may sample it?'

Tommy looked around the tent. 'And where would I find them, then, Maurice?'

Maurice shook his head, 'My dear Thomas, you truly need to open your ears a bit more. When I said crystal glasses, what I meant was anything we can drink out, of including those wooden cups there on the honourable Major's desk.'

Tommy hopped off the bed and walked over to retrieve the cups. As he picked them up, he noticed the Surgeon Major's journal open. He had a quick glance and found that Preston had once again written something about him.

21 July 1880. Subject: Male, approx. 20–25 years.
I have now ascertained that the subject is one Thomas Evans, Private, formerly of the Fusiliers. He apparently transferred to the 66th Foot whilst in India. This information I have yet to corroborate. I thought the young man was making progress, but it seems he still has the odd bout of psychosis, in that he continues to display a detachment with reality. If he has not improved within the next few days, I will be forced to have him relieved of duty and returned forthwith to Kandahar and then back to India for further treatment. I will continue to monitor his behaviour.

That's not good, thought Tommy. He walked back to his bed, handed Maurice the cups and sat down.

'Well, I must say, you appear extraordinarily misanthropic considering I have just unveiled a short term restorative to our ills,' intoned Maurice.

Tommy did not reply, as his mind was in turmoil about the consequences of the Major's journal. *Shit! What the hell am I gonna do? I need to get home! Shit! Home, now where the hell is that? Mum and Dad haven't even been born yet, or Granddad Stan. Think! What are you gonna do?*

While Tommy had been lost in thought, Maurice had pulled the cork from the bottle, poured two healthy measures into the cups and passed one to Tommy. He looked at him thoughtfully few moments.

'You seem distracted, Thomas.'

Tommy looked at him. 'Sorry, I was just thinking.'

'An overrated pastime. About what, pray?'

'About how the hell I'm gonna get out of here and back to where I came from, Maurice, because you know I don't belong here.' He looked at the floor. 'I don't!'

'Alright, old bean, now don't fret so. I'm sure the two of us can divine this conundrum, but for the immediate future, let us toast our good fortune at not having to labour out there in that furnace.' He indicated to the tent entrance.

Alright, Tommy thought, *just gotta go with the flow*, and he downed the cognac in one, which he regretted five seconds later as the liquid burned its way to his gut. He coughed with gusto.

Maurice chuckled, 'Well, if you throw it down your neck like some backstreet ruffian, that's the result. This nectar is far too saintly to be gormandised like that.'

Coughing again, Tommy said, 'Speak bloody English, will ya.'

'You have to take it steady, Thomas. It's not some cheap ale, you know.'

The coughing subsided, and Tommy held out his cup for another drink.

'Aha, it seems my elixir is doing its job. But be warned, my friend, this mellifluous intoxicant can surprise even the hardiest dipsomaniac.'

Tommy stared at Maurice. 'If you're gonna use big words, mate, then this chat is going to last a helluva long time, because I haven't the foggiest about what you're on about, *old bean*!'

'Very well. As you say, Thomas, I shall endeavour – sorry, try, to limit my vocabulary to something more unambiguous to suit your simpler tastes, no offence intended.'

'None taken, old boy, and I know what bloody endeavour means. I'm not thick, you know. Now fill that cup up, that stuff's not bad.'

With a smile, Maurice refilled Tommy's cup and his own, then he stoppered the bottle and returned it to his bag. 'So, my friend, do you have a plan as to your unusual predicament?'

Tommy sipped his drink this time. It still burned its way down his throat, but felt soothing. He smacked his lips. 'That is quite good Maurice, really good, in fact.' Then he shook his head.

'No, I don't actually, but I was thinking that I can't sit in here playing the nutter or they'll ship me off to India. At least that's what it said in the doc's diary over there.' He indicated the Major's desk with a nod of his head. 'So I was thinking "when in Rome" and all that, and trying to fit in a bit until I wake up, if you know what I mean.'

'You still think you're asleep, then. Very well, seeing that I am a part of your vagary, I shall offer my services as a guide through this torment of yours. How say you to that, old man?'

'Thanks, Maurice, that would be a big help.' He smiled at his new friend, who politely inclined his head. 'I think I have to have a look outside, though; I don't actually want to, but it needs to be done.'

Maurice slipped off his bed. His knees wobbled for a moment, but then he straightened. 'Very well, Thomas, let us take this road together,' and he indicated toward the tent opening.

Tommy hesitated. He didn't want this dream to get any bigger, but he had to see what was outside. Yet still he could not move.

'Just a quick peek, that is all, Thomas. Then back to our beds and my delicious elixir.' He indicated for Tommy to take the lead. 'After you, old man.'

Tommy moved towards the opening; the noises from outside the tent seemed to grow more terrifying with each step. Sweat broke out on his forehead and terrifying childhood thoughts played in his mind, the times his friends used to dare him to open the door to the cellar knowing full well that the beast that lurked inside would drag him to his death. He stopped before the opening, shaking slightly.

'All you have to do, Thomas, is open the flap and all will be revealed,' said Maurice, standing by his side.

Tommy reached a shaking hand out towards the flap, stopped halfway, then continued. He grabbed hold of a piece of rope attached to the edge, tensed, held his breath, and thought, *Should I do it slowly or snatch it open?* Just at that moment, he heard a snuffling sound. Confused, he looked down and saw a large pair of brown eyes looking up at him. Startled, he dropped the rope and stepped back, and for a split second it was the beast from the cellar come to get him.

'Well hello there, Fido,' said Maurice.

Tommy realised after a moment that it wasn't the beast but a dog, a medium-sized dirty-white, fluffy dog with tan ears. And a playful one at that, by the look of it, as he or she barked, turned and flew back through the opening.

'Isn't that lovely? You seemed to have made a new friend already,' said Maurice.

Tommy smiled at him, reached for the flap and pulled it aside, and was blinded by sunshine. He was taken aback for a moment and blinked hard to try and focus. As the scene before him started to materialise, he felt his legs start to wobble; he felt dizzy with the magnitude of what he was seeing. A hand grasped his elbow to steady him.

'Easy now, Thomas, I don't think I have the strength to pick you up if you fall,' whispered Maurice.

Tommy turned his head away from the scene outside, a scene of hundreds of tents stretching into the distance, of men – soldiers, most of them carrying out every sort of imaginable task – smoke from camp fires, shouting, laughing; he even saw a couple of children running in and out of the tents.

Cannons in the distance, rows of cannons, horses everywhere, tethered in enclosures; Indians, there were Indians also, some in uniform, some not, some idly chatting with each other, some bent over large cooking pots, stirring the contents.

'Maurice,' said Tommy in a whisper. 'It's real, it's all bloody real.'

Chapter 6
The Camp

After Tommy had managed to gulp down another cup of cognac, stop shaking and stop repeatedly pointing towards the entrance of the tent Maurice had managed to get him back onto the bed and calm down a little.

'Feeling any better now, Thomas?'

'Oh shit, Maurice. You know what, I still thought this was some massive joke the lads were playing on me, like maybe they had gotten actors in or something, you know, to make it convincing.' He shook his head and felt like crying. 'Maurice, have you seen that out there? That's a real army camp, I mean, not a modern one, but an old one. Shit, you know, like one you'd see in a period drama or Sharpe or something.'

'Thomas, my dear chap, I would love to understand what you are trying to say, but just to be clear on this, I have no idea what you're talking about. You might as well be speaking the local dialect, for the sense you're making.' He looked at Thomas with pity. 'Now see here, Thomas, you certainly ought to get a grip, you know. I can only help you if you endeavour to help yourself. Have another drop of this,' he said, and indicated the now half-empty bottle of cognac.

Tommy took another large swig and tried to relax a little. He could feel the alcohol starting to work. His muscles were softening, and after a few minutes of controlling his breathing, the situation didn't seem quite so grim. Well, not if you compare it to death anyway.

Maurice gave him a shrewd look. 'Thomas, are you quite sure this isn't some criterion for myself by our friend the Surgeon

Major? Because, if it is, I can assure you now, my disingenuous highbinder, that I will not fall for your little codification!'

'Now who's talking crap,' replied Tommy. 'Why don't you stop showing off, dictionary boy, and talk normal, eh?'

Maurice sat on his bed. 'So be it. Then is this some sort of test on me by the good Major? Just because I had some sort of fever on the way here doesn't make me mad, you know, and trying out this preposterous story on me to see if I would fall for it, well, it won't work, damn you. I am as fit as a butcher's hog.'

'Dog,' said Tommy.

'Pardon?'

'You mean dog. It's "fit as a butcher's dog."'

'That's what I said.'

'No, you said hog.' Tommy started to smile; he had noticed Maurice's cheeks had started to flush. *It's the drink*, he thought.

'Hog, dog, it makes no difference, as they are both quadrupeds, in any case.'

Tommy could see that Maurice was becoming a little worse for wear, so decided to end the drinking session. 'A toast,' he said and held up his cup. 'The Queen.'

'The Queen,' said Maurice, and both took a large swig of the fiery liquid. Maurice belched and said, 'A toast,' and held up his cup.

Tommy followed suit.

'To Joseph. May all his dreams come true, the good for nothing shit!' They both fell back onto the beds, laughing so hard they both produced tears.

Just then Major Preston entered the tent, and without as much as a glance, went straight to his table, opened his journal, picked up his quill and dipped it in a little bottle of ink and started writing.

The two friends looked at each other with a barely suppressed giggle. They shrugged and sat up on their beds, looking at Preston.

After a minute or so, and without looking up Preston, stopped writing, carefully placed his quill on the desk next to the ink pot, closed his journal and placed his hands on the desk in front of him. 'I will assume,' he said slowly, 'that your parents did not inform you that it is rude to stare.'

Before Tommy could say anything, Maurice said, 'I do apologise, Major Preston, sir, you are quite right, it is rude to stare. But you have piqued our curiosity with the, well, sombre appearance, if you don't mind my saying so.'

Preston turned and looked at Maurice, and held his gaze for some moments.

'You are remarkably astute, Mr Rayner, as always, and yes, I am a little out of sorts.'

'May I be so bold as to the reason, sir?'

Preston nodded to himself and stood. 'Yes,' he said, 'you may,' and walked over to Maurice's bedside.

'I have recently returned from visiting some of the men from the 66th, who have been attached to the smoothbore battery, and the reason, I think I mentioned it, was a suspected case of cholera. Well, after examination, I found it was not cholera but fatigue caused by hunger, little water and forced marching across this God forsaken hell.' Preston took a breath, and with an angry edge to his voice said, 'I have recently returned from giving my findings to one of General Burrows's staff, asking that the men be given enough water and time to recuperate, but I was informed that the British Army does not show weakness at the first sign of adversity. Apparently we will shortly be engaged with the enemy, and *that* is when it will be slightly uncomfortable for the men.'

'Ah,' said Maurice.

'Ah, indeed,' said Preston.

Tommy was just about to ask what enemy they were shortly to engage when Preston frowned and, with his nose slightly raised, started to sniff the air like a hunting dog.

'What is that smell?' asked Preston.

'Oh, I do apologise, sir,' said Maurice. 'Must have been the nosh the wallah gave me. My stomach is terribly upset, you know.'

Tommy snorted a laugh through his nose, but was silenced quickly by the look from Preston.

'That is not flatulence, Mr Rayner.'

Tommy was bursting to laugh and had to look at the ground to keep from doing so.

'If I am not too mistaken, that is the smell of alcohol.' And with that, he looked at the two friends one at a time. 'If I find, gentlemen, that you two have been at my medicinal liquor stock, there will be hell to pay. Do I make myself clear?'

The two friends looked at each other and then cast their eyes down to the floor.

'Perhaps I should fetch the Sergeant Major and he can make some enquiries.'

Maurice sighed. 'The alcohol is mine, sir. It has travelled with me from London,' he said, and he pulled the bottle from his bag.

Preston raised his eyebrows. 'Would that be a bottle of Hardy's you have, Mr Rayner?'

'Why yes, sir, it is.' And, seeing his chance, said, 'Would you care for a nip?'

'You know, it *has* been a somewhat tiring day.' He turned on the spot, walked over to his desk, opened his ornate case, dug around in the bottom of it for a moment and produced a glass tumbler. He blew some dust off it, picked up his stool and walked back to Maurice's bedside, where he sat and held out his glass to Maurice. 'An exceedingly tiring day indeed,' he said with a small smile.

The rest of the day was a blur for Tommy. Not only did they finish the cognac, but the Major disappeared for a short time and then returned with a bottle of scotch from his medicinal stock. Tommy spent the entire afternoon and evening listening to the two officers reminisce about India, England and going to school at Harrow, and how Maurice was a budding cricket star. Tommy's eyes grew heavy. He lay down on his back, and, still listening, fell asleep.

Pain.

Not again! thought Tommy, as he opened his eyes. This time, though, the view was not of a horse's arse or a sexy, hairy man-woman, but of Maurice in the other bed next to him. He was lying on his side facing Tommy with his mouth open, and there was a long line of spittle dribbling from his mouth and onto the lumpy pillow. Even though he had a headache (again), he couldn't help but smile; Maurice had certainly lost his dignified look now.

He lifted his head to scan the tent, and was surprised to find the Major slumped over his desk. *Bloody hell*, he thought, *I missed a lively session here*. Very slowly, he sat up in the bed and tried to gather his thoughts, but found they were a jumble. He suddenly realised he hadn't had a drink like that since England. *No wonder my head's thumping*, he thought.

He needed to piss and badly. He couldn't remember the last time he had been, and looked over to the tent opening. *Bollocks*. He was going to have to go outside, and was tempted for a moment to wake Maurice to go with him.

'What the hell am I thinking,' he said to himself. 'Am I gonna get him to hold it as well?' He climbed out of bed and gave himself a once over; he was still wearing the dirty greyish trousers and vest-type garment he had woken up in yesterday – or the day before, he couldn't recall. Time had stood still for him.

He looked over at the two officers and still couldn't believe any of this was real, but how could a dream be so vivid and long-lasting? With tentative steps, he walked over to the tent opening and stood before it. He listened for a moment and found that yesterday's noise was substantially reduced. He surmised that it may be morning, as the light in the tent was quite dim. *Or is it dusk and just the same day over and over?* He shivered as he remembered that movie *Groundhog Day*, where the guy keeps reliving the same day over and over again. *But*, he thought, *where is the beautiful woman in my repeating day, because if whoever's controlling this thing thinks I will end up trying it on with the lovely Arun, well, they've got another thing coming*. He chuckled at this and decided that he was going mad after all.

He reached for the flap of the opening and pulled it open just a little. *Wow! What a scene!* he thought. The sun was just rising over a mountain range in the distance and was casting an orange red glow over the massive camp site. Mist hovered over the lines of tents, and he realised that his view was from a raised vantage point. The sight was breathtaking! And it was incredible to believe he was seeing a military camp from the 1880s.

His full bladder was forgotten for the moment, so he squatted down to survey the scene. There were a few bodies moving around in the mist – and smoke, he realised – for he saw a few men, Indians by the look of them, starting fires. *Cooking fires probably*, he thought.

More images were coming to him now: horses, quite a few of them, and the gun carriages he had seen yesterday, last night, whenever. His school days were coming back to him too, the history lessons from Mr Roberts, pouring over books in the library and reading about the wonderful tales of bravery of the British Army in Africa, fighting the Zulus, or in the Anglo– Afghan wars. Everything was coming back to him, the endless images of the Red Coats fighting off hoards of tribesmen or Cossacks or Boers or French Garde Impériale. *Dad would love this*, he thought, as he wiped at the tears forming in his eyes. Then he stood, took a deep breath and walked through the entrance.

The heat hit him. *Jeeeeze*, he thought, *that mist won't last long*. He started to look for a toilet, but couldn't see anything remotely like a loo. *Idiot!* he thought after a few moments. *What do you expect, soft toilet roll as well? It will be a ditch, won't it, with maybe a cover and separate stalls, or it could just be a bucket.* Tommy was ready to burst. He looked around the back of the tent and found a small tree clinging to life.

'Aha!'

He trotted over to it and spent one or two minutes struggling with his trousers. 'Stupid sodding things,' he said as he got the last button undone. He then spent the next few moments looking up at the sunrise with half-lidded eyes and a stupid smile on his face. He frowned as a thought came to him: *What if I need to shit?* He would have to dig a hole, and he didn't relish the thought of trying to wipe his arse with anything rougher than the cardboard they used here. Just as he was finishing emptying his bladder, the silence was ripped apart by a bugle.

'Shit, shit,' he said, as he desperately tried to do up his trousers while trotting back to the opening of the tent. 'That was the Reveille! Everyone will be awake in a minute.'

He managed to do up the last button as he he stepped into the entrance of the tent. At that moment, he glanced back at the camp and saw, at the nearest cooking fire, an old man leaning over a pot, stirring the contents. The old man stopped, looked up at Tommy and smiled. Tommy frowned. Had he seen this guy somewhere before? He was about to beckon him over when there was an almighty groan from inside the tent. He turned and found Major Preston sitting up at his desk and rubbing his temples with the palms of his hands. Tommy swung back to the old man but he was gone, replaced by a young Indian soldier. He poked his head out and looked around, but it was no use; there were thousands of men now vacating their tents, stretching and yawning in the early morning sun. Still confused by what he had just seen, he let the flap fall back and returned to his bed.

'I despise that infernal racket,' moaned Maurice as he rolled onto his back. He pushed himself onto his elbows and looked over blearily at Tommy. 'Well, I must say, you look decidedly sprightly this morning, Thomas. However, the perpetual look of confusion is starting to be a bore.'

'Good morning to you too, ya miserable git,' replied Tommy. He chuckled to himself. 'If you can't handle your drink, mate, then don't do it.'

Maurice flopped down onto his back and sighed. 'Sorry, old chap, but I think the gentlemen with the hammers inside my skull are going to it with far too much delectation, what.'

'Yeah, well, ok then, if you say so. I think we're all feeling a little worse for wear this morning.' He nodded in the direction of Preston. 'Take a look at the Major over there.'

Maurice looked over at Preston and found him sitting at his desk with his head in his hands. 'My dear Major, are you feeling unwell?'

'Mr Rayner, your aphorism and sarcasm are not wanted at this time, so please tread particularly carefully before you continue,' Preston said in a gravelly voice.

'Sir, I was only concerned as to your felicity, given the aberrant locus you have adopted.'

'Yes, well, that will be quite enough of that, thank you, Lieutenant. Now if you will excuse me, I have matters to attend to.' Preston stood a little shakily and, looking rather green, made his way out of the tent entrance. A second or so later, the Tommy and Maurice could hear the sound of him retching.

'Oh dear, the poor Major sounds rather poorly. I wonder if he needs a doctor?'

'Don't take the piss, Maurice. Preston's all right as officers go.'

'I was effecting a jape, Thomas. I know the Major is a thoroughly likeable chap. And is that what "take the piss means," to make fun of?'

'Yeah, something like that.'

'You must teach me some of this strange language you use, Thomas. If we are to be compatriots, we must learn to converse a little better, what.'

'OK.'

'There you go again. What is "OK"?'

'Err, it means all right and can be used for, I don't know, acceptable and other shit like that.' He stood. 'Now do me a favour, Maurice, and tell me what my uniform looks like and where I can find it.'

'Should be at the end of the bed in a rough wooden chest. But why do you want to know where it is, Thomas?'

'Because, me old mate, I'm gonna have a little stroll round the camp. It's not every day you get a chance to walk around a genuine nineteenth-century army camp, and if I am asleep right now, I might wake up without doing it. And you know how hard it is to get back into a dream once you've woken up.'

Tommy said this while unpacking the uniform he had found in the chest at the bottom of his bed, pith helmet included.

Maurice swung his legs out and moved to the end of his bed, unpacked his own uniform and started to remove his bed clothes.

'What are you doing?'

'You said, Thomas, that you are from the future. Yet you didn't tell me when in the future.'

Tommy stopped what he was doing, 'OK, Maurice, I'm from the twenty-first, well, no, actually I'm from the twentieth-century. I was born in 1989, but it's the twenty-first right now.' He gave Maurice a resigned look. 'Now you know, mate. I'm bonkers!'

'Well, my twenty-first century friend, if you're going to go for a stroll out there, you will need a nineteenth-century chaperone. We don't want you getting into any unfortunate predicaments, do we? Besides, I am famished. What say we go and procure a bite to eat.'

'Thanks, Maurice,' said Tommy with forced gratitude. Although he didn't say it, he wasn't looking forward to it really. He checked the uniform and found it was quite basic: matching trousers and tunic, with buttons up the front and a waistband that came up nearly to his armpits. The boots looked as if they were ready to fall apart, and the dirty grey, bandage-type gaiters were, well, they looked like gaiters. *My God*, he thought. He was starting to sweat and he hadn't put half of it on yet. He looked over at Maurice, who was humming as he dressed himself.

'Maurice, will you give me a hand with this, mate?'

'Certainly, old chap.'

Twenty minutes later, they were dressed. Tommy was starting to feel the heat already.

'How the hell can you march and fight in this get up? It's crap, there's no movement in it and it's itchy as hell.'

'Thomas, my dear chap, how could you possibly go into battle not looking the part, eh? It's what separates the British Army from all those other savages out there in their delicate and cool cotton garb. We are the Red Coats – well, khaki at the moment – scourge of all those with poor dress sense.'

Tommy tried on the helmet and found it was a perfect fit. He took it off again and checked the inside, and found a name scrawled in the lining. *T Evans*.

'What the fuck!' he exclaimed and, dropping the helmet as though it had given him an electric shock, he stepped backwards a few paces.

'Thomas, whatever is the matter?'

Tommy couldn't breathe. *How can that be my name?* he thought. He was trembling from shock; he tried to speak but it came out in a squeak.

Maurice took two quick steps and took hold of Tommy by the shoulders, who had started to sway, and guided him to the stool by his bed. He sat with a thud.

'Thomas,' he said. 'Thomas.'

Tommy looked up at him, the shock evident in his eyes.

'How can my name be in that helmet, Maurice?' He paused for a moment. Then he said, angrier, 'How the fuck did my name get in that helmet? Did you put it in there? Preston? That twat, when I was on that cart? Come on, Maurice, you can tell me now. I had a terrific time but the game's over.'

'Over!'

Maurice took an involuntary step back and looked aghast at Tommy.

'Thomas, I can assure you, as a friend, no one put your name in the helmet. It was already there when you were brought in. I swear to you, no one has tampered with your belongings since you arrived.'

He was breathing heavy now, his eyes bulging with anger and fear.

'Was it that arsehole Watson? It had to be.' Tommy was confused for a moment. 'But I don't remember telling him my name or anything.'

Just then Arun entered carrying a jug of water.

'Good mornings.'

He wandered over to the desk looking for the wooden cups, and frowned when he couldn't find them. He turned to the two men. 'Pardons but have you seen wooden cups for drinking water, please?'

Maurice nodded toward the floor by his bed.

Arun smiled and moved forward to pick them up. Suddenly Tommy stood and grabbed him by the shirt. 'What's my name?'

'Pardons, Private Sahib, I will fetch water now,' said Arun with a sudden look of fear.

'I said, what's my fucking NAME?' Tommy thundered, spittle flying out of his mouth.

'I, I— I,' stuttered Arun, who was now trying to walk backwards.

Tommy felt a hand on his arm, and a dead calm voice said, 'Thomas, he is just a wallah, for heaven's sake. He makes the food, fetches water, a general help for the Major. He wouldn't know anything even if it were to slap him in the face, and he's terrified, look at him.'

Tommy's eyes cleared and he could see that the Arun was on the brink of crying.

'Shit, Arun, I'm sorry, I, please—' He let go and the wallah ran from the tent.

'Don't apologise to the help, Thomas, it won't do. Now then, let's have a look, shall we?' He picked up the helmet and looked inside. 'Oh yes, I see now, I can see why you are so angry, yes indeed.'

'Do ya see what I mean, Maurice?' said Tommy with hope in his voice.

'Absolutely, old chap. Some bally fool has gone and written your name inside your bloody helmet.' He tossed it back to Tommy. 'Disgraceful behaviour, deserves at least thirty strokes of the Cat!' With that he placed his own helmet on his head, turned and walked to the entrance, and without looking back said, 'I quite fancy a little peregrination myself now. Will you juxtapose with me?' and walked out of the tent.

Tommy thought quickly; he didn't want to be left alone in the tent, so he rammed his helmet on his head and followed Maurice out into the sunshine.

The glare from the sun was powerful enough to make Tommy shield his eyes for a moment, as he stopped just outside the entrance and squinted, looking for Maurice. *God, I feel like a helpless child! This is ridiculous; it's just a dream after all.* With that comforting thought, he trotted after Maurice, who was walking down the small rise on which the hospital tent was pitched. Catching up and falling into step with him, Tommy took in his surroundings. The different smells assailing his senses were incredible, let alone the scenes. Smoke, spices, meat cooking, shit! *Human*, he thought, for it didn't have that dungy overtone.

Sweat, tobacco smoke… this last smell made him crave a ciggy, an addiction he had only recently managed to kick. They walked past tents with the occupants doing all sorts of tasks, from peeling spuds to polishing buttons to cleaning rifles. *Big bloody rifles as well*, he thought. *I wouldn't fancy trying to fight holding one of those things up. Give me the SA80 any day.*

Indians, there were a lot of Indians as well, with huge turbans. *This must be an Indian regiment*, he thought.

'Maurice,' he spoke out of the side of his mouth, 'is this an Indian regiment?'

'These are some of the men from the 30th Bombay Infantry, Thomas, and the Jacob's Rifles, that's those chaps over there,' he said, and indicated with a nod of his head to where a column of Indian soldiers were marching. 'And those to our left over there are the Grenadiers. Now please stop gawking like a curious child, Thomas, and try to look dignified.'

But Thomas couldn't help but gawk. It was like stepping onto the set of a movie, only without the cameras and other paraphernalia. He did manage to close his mouth, though his head kept bobbing all around like a meercat. The Grenadiers, he noticed, were just like the modern version, all big lads, six-foot-plus, most of them. They looked a lot more relaxed than the guys from the infantry. *Typical*, he thought.

They continued walking past row after row of tents, carts, cooking fires and tepee-style stacks of weapons. Tommy's eyes had started to water with all the smoke, and he rubbed at the irritation.

Maurice looked at him. 'I know, Thomas, I know, it brings a tear to my eye as well, every time I look upon this well-oiled machine.'

'I'm not crying, Maurice, you fool. It's this bloody smoke. How do you put up with it?'

'Put up with it? Why, how else are we supposed to cook food, heat water and what not?'

'Oh, yeah.' Tommy realised he was getting a little hot and thirsty. 'Maurice, any chance we could stop for a drink? Is there a NAAFI or something round here? I'm dying of thirst, mate.'

'Firstly, old chap, I have no idea what a NAAFI is, and secondly, if we need a drink of water, we use our canteens. However, as I forgot to replenish mine own, I will allow you that small erratum, what.'

Maurice looked around for a few seconds, then said, 'You there,' to a young Indian man in modest clothes who was hunched over a large copper urn.

The man stood, trotted over and bowed. 'Lieutenant Sahib, you are wanting a cup of most delicious tea?'

'Not at the moment, my dear man, but would you have any clean water? If so, would you be so kind as to fill our canteens? There's a good chap, what.'

Maurice removed his canteen from his webbing belt, and, indicating for Tommy to do the same, handed them both to the chai wallah.

'Oh yes, Sahib, one moment please.' He turned and trotted off towards a large barrel.

'Well, Thomas, what say you to our little camp? The British Army can make a home anywhere in the world, you know.'

'Amazing, really amazing Maurice.' Tommy was watching a couple of big Indian Grenadiers doing stretching exercises in front of their tent, and thought briefly of Arun. 'Oh for Christ sake,' he said to himself, remembering his dream.

Maurice followed Tommy's gazing and frowned; then, after a few moments, it dawned on him why Tommy quickly looked at the ground.

'Ah, I see,' Maurice chuckled. 'Thomas, my dear chap, I'm sure the lovely Miss Arun will forgive you in time, and then you may resume you attempts at courtship.'

'Piss off.'

The chai wallah returned with their canteens and stood watching while they slaked their thirst.

'Well done, you may go about your business,' Maurice said to the wallah, who bobbed his head a couple of times and returned to his tea urn.

Tommy drank half of his canteen in one, screwed the metal top back into place and returned it to his belt. *That's better*, he thought, and while Maurice continued to sip his water he scanned the camp, trying to avoid the stretching Grenadiers. It was truly incredible to behold, like stepping into an old picture. The sounds of tools, of laughing, of orders being shouted filled Tommy's ears, and he noticed the Cavalry in the distance, riding at the head of a dust cloud. He noticed also, when he did a 180-degree turn, that there seemed to be outriders all around the sprawling camp. *Recon*, his soldier instincts told him, *or scouts in this age, keeping vigil. In fact there was probably a network of scouts stretching many miles in all directions.* His thoughts were broken by Maurice.

'Don't look now. Here comes Major Oliver.'

Tommy turned to see where Maurice was gazing and saw three officers walking toward them.

'Now look here, Thomas, don't speak until spoken to and do not, I repeat, do not start rambling about death, dreams and time travel. This man is an ignorant bore and has undoubtedly no sense of humour whatsoever. He will have you on a charge before you know what's happened, insane or not. And for God's sake, man, come to attention,' he hissed under his breath.

Tommy shot to attention just as the officers arrived.

'Ah, Lieutenant Rayner. I see you are making a recovery,' boomed the officer who was obviously Major Oliver. Tommy did not look at him but stared at his helmet instead. There was an accent underneath the clipped English that Tommy couldn't put his finger on, Scottish, maybe, or Irish.

'I am making a speedy recovery, sir, thank you, although Surgeon Major Preston insists on keeping me immured in his dungeon, which I find dreadfully bromidic by the way, and that is why, sir, I borrowed Private Evans here, who is recovering from wounds sustained in our recent skirmish at Girishk, to escort me on a little constitutional.'

Tommy could feel the Major's eyes appraising him but still did not look in his face.

'Is that so, Lieutenant? Well then, what befell you, Private, in our tryst with the levies?'

Tommy did not look away from the helmet. 'I had a bump on me head, Major, sir, and it was combusted, Major, sir.'

Oliver sniffed. 'Quite.' He looked back to Maurice. 'You know Captains Garratt and McMath, I presume, Lieutenant?'

Maurice smiled at the other officers. 'I have had the fortunate pleasure, sir, yes,' and he nodded to both, who returned the nod with genuine smiles.

Oliver continued, 'There is more than a fair chance we will be striking camp soon. There have been reports that Ayub Khan's army has crossed the Helmand en masse, so we may try and intercept it. We are just on our way to inspect E battery to make sure everything is in place and ready to move, although I'm sure Blackwood has it in hand, he always does. Right, can't stand around all day nattering like old women. Some of us have jobs to do, ain't that right, Lieutenant?' And with that, he marched off between the tents. The two Captains, Garratt and McMath, smiled and nodded to both men, and Garratt even patted Tommy on the shoulder as he went past, following the Major.

They could both hear the Major shouting at the chai wallah. 'No, I don't want any of your delicious bloody tea.'

'What an insufferable oaf that man is,' said Maurice, and Tommy nodded his agreement.

'Thomas, combusted, really!'

'Sounded OK though, didn't it!'

Chapter 7
Fight

The sun was climbing higher and the heat of the day was beginning to take its toll, especially on the British regiment. The Indians, by contrast, although used to a different sort of heat, were coping much better than their counterparts. The thin mist of early morning had dissipated suddenly and only the smoke from the cooking fires was left hovering over the camp like London smog. Soldiers were still going about their business though, and there was an air of anticipation as the rumour of an impending battle with Ayub Khan's forces spread quickly round the camp.

Some men, usually the younger ones, were all bravado, puffing their chests and recounting stories of past prowess in whatever battles they'd seen, including bar-room brawls. The older soldiers went about their business with quiet reflection. The ones that had already been involved in engagements were now thinking of home, children, wives or even mistresses; they knew what to expect and so resigned themselves to cleaning their kit, making sure their weapons were in perfect working order and telling the younger ones to do the same. Sergeants walked amongst them, berating here and there, giving encouragement to others, telling the men that the quicker that they get this job done, the quicker they could get back to India, and then home.

Later in the afternoon, Tommy and Maurice were sitting on stools outside the hospital tent, eating a bowl of meat broth that Arun had brought them. Although still wary of another outburst from Tommy, Arun was well schooled in the unusual ways of the British Sahibs, and dutifully carried on with his daily chores. Tommy had taken off his tunic and helmet after asking Maurice if he would draw attention to himself.

'Not at all, old man. Remember, we are ephemera of the good Surgeon Major and, given that we are convalescing, we are not on the roll, so to speak.'

So Tommy now sat, contentedly eating his lunch – *it must be lunch*, he thought, because he got it for breakfast as well – and watched the hustle and bustle of the camp. He was watching the Grenadiers. One of them stripped to the waist and was stretching, while others had gathered round, forming a rough square.

'What's going on down there, then, Maurice?' and indicated toward the group with a nod of his head.

Maurice turned on his stool and looked down at the men. 'Ah,' he said, 'seems very much like we are going to see a bit of pugilism, old man,' and he turned fully round on his stool to watch.

'Is that allowed, mate? Isn't it against regulations or something?'

'Not at all, my friend. The General likes the sport, so he avidly encourages it as long as the Queensberry Rules are followed, and the match is refereed so nobody gets hurt, of course. Can't say I would like to be in there with that Indian fellow though. He looks rather herculean, does he not?'

'Yeah, he's a big lad all right.' Tommy watched the Indian, wearing nought but a loin cloth, walk around the ring flexing his muscular arms and shoulders. His leg muscles were so large they looked like tree trunks. *He must be at least 6'2" or 6'3" and extremely fit by the look of him*, Tommy thought. The man had an arrogant look behind the beard he was sporting, and from what he could see of a scarred face, Tommy didn't envy his opponent one bit.

'Aha, and here comes our champion of the 66th, Private Davis,' said Maurice. 'A likeable chap, albeit he is as stupid as he is big.'

Tommy watched Davis walk into the square of bodies. He was perhaps touching six feet and was muscular under a thin layer of fat. He had a belly on him too, which was hanging over his issue trousers. His hair was cut short at the back and sides, with a centre part and a massive handlebar moustache. What the attraction to these bushy moustaches was was beyond Tommy. You couldn't even see Davis's mouth. But he did look remarkably confident given the size of his opponent, and he started to limber himself up.

As the fighters were getting their gloves on, a Sergeant entered the square, a man from the 66th. *The referee,* Tommy supposed, *and a beard like ZZ Top!* He called the boxers to him in the centre, and by the way he was gesticulating, it appeared he was telling them to fight fairly. He kept pointing at his mouth, his head and his groin.

'I do believe we're in for a treat, Thomas, a clash of the Titans if ever there was one, what.'

Tommy was interested now and stood to watch. As the fighters moved to opposite corners, they stared each other down. The Indian's face was impassive, but Davis, Tommy noticed, must be smiling, as his moustache was curving upwards. The referee stepped into the middle, sliced his hand through the air, shouted 'Begin,' and moved back. Davis came out of his corner like a bull, his hands raised only to waist height. He moved up to the Indian, who had only taken a couple of steps, and started throwing punches at the Grenadier's head. For such a large man, the Grenadier moved with incredible speed, dodging Davis's gloved fists as though he were throwing them in slow motion.

Left, right, straight, nothing was catching him, and he suddenly stepped to the side and jabbed a left into Davis's face, who stumbled backwards, off balance. But instead of following up, the Indian walked calmly around him, face impassive, and Tommy thought the Grenadier had his guard up where it belonged, in front of his face. Davis shook his head and resumed the onslaught with a barrage of punches, but again couldn't connect with the other man's head. He then tried for a body shot but received a straight cross in the dead centre of his forehead and landed on his arse with a great thud. The crowd of soldiers, a mix of Grenadier and the 66th, were roaring their fighters on with gusto. Tommy realised he was silently willing Davis to get his guard up. The Private got to his feet and shook his head again, but this time his legs had started to wobble and he staggered a little. The Indian, instead of taking advantage of this, calmly walked around Davis, who was probably seeing double from that last punch.

Snap! The Indians left glove snaked out and caught Davis on the nose, not enough to put him down again but enough to start his nose bleeding. Snap! Another jab, straight to the right eye. Davis swung and caught air as the Indian ducked and planted a right into the other's stomach. From where he and Maurice were standing, Tommy could hear the breath leave the man, and winced at the fighter's pain. Again the Indian continued to circle as Davis tried unsuccessfully to catch his breath.

'I say, that Grenadier chap is rather splendid, don't you think, Thomas? Thomas?'

'Hmm? Oh yeah, he is,' replied Tommy, who was deep in thought. 'He's just playing with him Maurice, making him look like an arsehole in front of his mates and the regiment. He's just gonna knock him about a bit before he finishes him, you watch.'

As Davis caught his breath and straightened up, he found the Grenadier standing directly in front of him. Tap, tap, tap, three quick-fire jabs straight to the Private's face, making him stagger backwards. The Indian stepped to the right and put another hook into the ribs. To his credit, Davis, still in pain from that last shot, tried another couple of punches, a left-right combo, and actually managed to catch the Grenadier with a glancing blow to the chin. Infuriated at having been caught, he stepped forward, and with blistering speed, landed three or four punches to the Private's now swelling face, then once again stepped out of reach.

Davis, with his eyes now swollen shut, attempted to throw a powerful right hand. He over balanced and his jaw connected with the Grenadier's right glove. He stood in the centre of the square, arms now completely dropped , out on his feet. Tommy was disgusted that it had gone this far. The Indian had been far too good for Davis, and he wished that the ref would stop it. Indeed, just as this thought came to him, the referee stepped forward to end the debacle, but before he could reach the centre, the Grenadier jumped forward and planted a thumping right straight into the other man's temple. Davis's legs folded like wet paper and he landed on his side, utterly unconscious, and the crowd roared with both glee and anger. Tommy was sickened. He sat back down.

'That was extremely entertaining, don't you think, Thomas?'

'No Maurice, it wasn't. It was disgusting and it should have been stopped after the first couple of minutes.'

'Stopped? Whatever for?

'So nobody gets too hurt, obviously.'

'Hurt? How stupid of me, I thought that was the whole purpose of throwing your fists at each other's faces!'

'Well, yeah it is, but you can get brain damage from taking too many punches and all that, and it was stupid to let that go so far. He could be seriously hurt down there.'

'Well, bless my soul, and there's me thinking that brain damage was a requisite before you were allowed to enter into that square.'

'You know what, bollocks to the lot of ya.' Tommy stood, angry and disgusted at what he had witnessed, and turned to enter the tent.

'Thomas! Really, if I'd thought you were such a sensitive soul, I wouldn't have allowed you to watch it. I thought you were a tough, twenty-first-century soldier and all that balderdash, what.'

Tommy gave him the finger and went inside the tent. He collapsed onto his bed, hot, sweaty, annoyed, confused and homesick, to name but a few.

'You're a tosser, Maurice, you know that?' he shouted, and he got even more wound up when he heard laughing outside. Tommy buried his head in the pillow and bit down on it to control his anger. After many thoughts of home, this place, this nightmare place, that dickhead of a Grenadier and giving Maurice a wicked slap, he drifted off to sleep.

When he woke it was gloomy in the tent, and the only source of light was a paraffin lamp on the Major's desk. He sat up, confused for a moment, and rubbed his eyes; and after a while, he remembered that afternoon, watching that Private get an unnecessary beating, and feeling like a wimpy child at the hand of Maurice's sarcasm.

'Fuck it,' he said to himself, and he slipped off the bed, stood and stretched. He was still wearing half his uniform as he made his way to the entrance of the tent. My *uniform!* he thought, *That's a laugh.* He popped his head out of the flaps and into a warm evening, the sun having only just disappeared behind some mountains in the distance. Maurice was sitting on a wooden fold-up chair and was talking to Major Preston, and both were seated around a little wooden table.

'Ah, Thomas, how delightful of you to join us,' said Maurice. Tommy could see that he had been drinking again.

'Good evening, Mr Evans,' said Preston. And Tommy noticed for the first time the real slight Irish lilt to his accent.

'Good evening, sir,' said Tommy. He didn't reply to or acknowledge Maurice.

'You will forgive me, gentlemen,' said Preston as he stood up. 'I have been summoned to attend the General's tent for dinner this evening and to hear reports of Mr Ayub Khan's movements. Though what that has to do with a surgeon attached to the 66th, I am unsure. But nevertheless, I must attend. A good evening to you both.' And he turned and walked away into the night.

There was an uncomfortable silence for a moment, until Maurice finally broke it.

'I am sorry, Thomas, if I offended you this afternoon. My humour sometimes gets the better of me and I am sure that in the twenty-first century, boxing is an uncouth and despicable pastime. Please forgive my somewhat trite humour.'

Tommy was unarmed straight away, because, although Maurice could be a complete upper-class, sarcastic, piss-taking twat, he was also highly likeable and had sincerity about him when he wasn't making fun.

'To tell you the truth, Maurice, boxing is massive in my time, a hugely popular multimillion-pound industry, and a skilled fighter is worth looking after. I accept your apology, mate.'

'Multimillion pounds, you say. We do have the same currency in the future, surely?' he said with a smile.

'Maurice, if I was to tell you what it's like in a hundred-odd years, even you will let them cart me off to a madhouse.'

'I believe you may be correct, old chap. Now sit you down, I have an ambrosial liquor here that I have fortunately come by with the help of a certain Captain I know, and it is awaiting your approval.'

Tommy sat on the opposite chair and accepted the glass Maurice offered. 'I don't know about you, but I'm sick to death of drinking out of wooden cups.' He then poured a golden liquid into Tommy's glass.

'To your very good health, old chap,' said Maurice, and he raised his glass.

'Cheers, Maurice.'

They sipped their drinks in silence for a few minutes and watched the camp, listening to its sounds; somebody was singing along to a guitar, a bawdy song involving a general's daughter and the gallows, and when it got to the chorus three or four others joined in. In the end, Tommy found himself tapping along to the tune.

'Harmonious bunch, wouldn't you say, Thomas?'

'Catchy tune, that,' Tommy said, and he wondered where the sound of the guitar was coming from; he tried to locate the direction but failed.

Just then Arun came up to the friends, carrying a wrapped cloth bundle which he placed on the table.

'Pardons, a message from the Captain Garratt Sahib. Message is please be enjoying, Lieutenant Rayner Sahib.' And with that he bowed quickly and attempted to leave. But before he got even a few feet, Tommy stopped him.

'Hang on, Arun. Listen, I'm sorry I frightened you. I didn't mean to, I apologise.'

Arun looked dumbfounded for a moment. 'No need apologies, Private Sahib. I is to blame, pardons.' He nodded and turned but Tommy refused to let him go.

'Wait, Arun, do me a favour, will you, and have a walk down there and see who's playing that guitar for me, please.'

Arun looked at Maurice for a split second and then nodded. 'Yes please,' he said, and wandered off to find the guitar player.

'Why the interest, then, Thomas?'

Tommy took a sip of the drink Maurice has poured him and found that it was another whisky, *and an exceedingly smooth malt at that*, he thought. *My god, if Granddad could see me now, drinking single malt from the nineteenth century, he would be well jealous.*

'Oh, I dunno, just a thought. Anyway, what's in the parcel, Maurice?'

Maurice unwrapped the cloth to reveal half a loaf of fresh bread and a large cut of roast pork.

'This, Thomas, is a return favour from the Gallant Captain Garratt. You see, when his friend Captain McMath was injured by a rather angry panther he was hunting, well, I managed to supply certain objects of a medicinal quality to help poor Mr McMath in his recovery. It's not a Roman Saturnalia, but it's all I could manage to appropriate at this time, courtesy of the General's table.'

Thomas's mouth started to water at the sight of the meat and bread. Bread!

'Maurice, it's fantastic but how did you manage to get,' he sniffed, 'fresh bread out here?'

'Well, the General likes his niceties, so he had a portable bread oven added to the baggage train. Not a crook idea, actually, especially when the likes of us can pilfer some of it, what.'

Tommy shook his head in wonder. 'You, Maurice, me old mate, are a genius.'

They both tucked into the feast, and it *was* a feast after the meat and potato slop they had been eating. After twenty minutes or so of silent eating while the sounds of the camp washed over them, Tommy sat back and rubbed his stomach, belched and smiled at Maurice.

Maurice sat back too, raised his glass in a silent toast to Tommy and took a healthy gulp.

'So, Thomas, now that we have gotten to know each other a little better and are now brothers in arms, will you not tell me what your future is like?'

'All right, Maurice, what do you wanna know?'

'Well, I don't know, why don't you tell me about yourself.'

Thomas took another gulp of whisky. 'Not that interesting, really. There's me, Mum, Dad and my little sister. I still live at home when I'm on leave, that's if I'm not away on holiday somewhere. We live on the Isle of Wight, my Mum's a nurse at the local NHS hospital and my Dad's a retired chippy. I did my A levels, then a small stint doing bar work, then building work. Wasted my time, actually, should have gone to university. But instead I joined the army, infantry, and when I get back, I'm gonna go for a stripe.'

Maurice sat dumbfounded. Even if he thought Tommy was sick and that this was all his delusion, he was surprised at how Tommy managed to think up all that hogwash on the spot. After a few moments, he decided to delve deeper. 'Thomas, what does NHS mean?'

'National Health Service.'

'And what is a National Health Service.'

Never having had to explain it before, Tommy paused for a moment. 'Well, you sort of pay your national insurance out of your wages and salaries, and that covers you if you, I dunno, need an operation or something, or you wanna get something fixed, or, you know, you need to go in to hospital for anything, really. There's an NHS hospital in all our cities, and doctors' surgeries and dentists.'

'Really?' Maurice said, not convinced. 'And what did you mean by "should have gone to university"?'

'Oh, well, I'd gotten all my GCSEs and A levels at school, so I was thinking of taking a History degree, or maybe Art, but you know how it is. I was a kid, I wanted money and holidays and a car, so I went and got work instead. Worst mistake ever, really.'

'You were going to go to university where, Oxford or Cambridge?' Maurice said with a smirk.

'Don't take the piss, Maurice, you said you wanted to hear about it.' Tommy took a swig of whisky. 'Now I could be blowing your mind with tales of aeroplanes and motorcars, couldn't I? How we don't use horses to pull our carts around anymore, haven't for about a hundred years or so. They move themselves by an engine and nearly everyone has got one.' He took a sip of his drink, and was amused to find Maurice was sitting with his mouth agape.

'Or planes, Maurice, huge metal birds with engines to power them. They can carry passengers across the Atlantic in a few hours, and some are used by the military, bombers, fighter planes. Submarines, they can travel under water and stay under for months on end. Do you see, Maurice, why I shouldn't tell you anything? We have even put men on the moon, Maurice.'

Tommy was thoroughly enjoying himself now, and he felt free talking about these things. 'That's right, on the moon. Taken there by rockets, whopping great rockets. That's only ninety years from now, mate. And let's not talk about computers, oh no, they control just about everything, from the cars to planes to mobile phones. Oh, I haven't mentioned phones, have I? Well, it's sort of a telegraph, Maurice, but it fits in the palm of your hand and you can talk through it to anyone, anywhere in the world at any time. And finally, mate, the nuclear bomb, a weapon so powerful that just one would level this area for a ten mile radius and kill every living thing.'

Tommy stopped, finished his drink and poured himself another.

Maurice was staring at him with what Tommy thought was scorn. Maurice coughed lightly and took a sip of his drink. Then he held it in his lap. 'Do you take me for a fool, Thomas? I thought we were friends, yet you take me for a fool.'

'What you on about, Maurice? You asked me to tell you, mate.'

'You think me illiterate, Thomas. You think you are the only one to have perused *Voyages Extraordinaires*, or other works of Mr Verne?'

'Oh for Christ's sake,' Tommy said, leaning forward. 'Maurice, do I or have I sounded like a common soldier from your time? Mate! I know maths, English, I'm not too shoddy at geography. I can speak basic French and German, and a little Spanish – well, I can ask for a pint of lager and a blow job, anyway. I know my history as well, though I'm a little rusty right now. I am a modern soldier, I can fight, read maps, do basic first aid. I know basic chemistry; give me the right household chemicals and I can make explosives. I can tell you scientific discoveries.' Maurice still looked unconvinced. Just then, Arun, who had been patiently waiting for Tommy to finish, stepped forward.

'Private Sahib, I am locating sitar for you,' he said, and he bobbed his head.

Tommy thought for a moment. 'Arun, can you tell whoever is playing that Lieutenant Rayner would like them to bring it to the hospital tent, and right now.'

Arun looked at Maurice, who rolled his eyes and nodded. 'Yes please, Sahib,' he said, and hurried off.

Tommy sat back in his chair and supped some more of the whisky; he could start to feel its effect and he felt rather content. Saying all those things to Maurice had, in a way, put him back in touch with reality, and now, he thought, he would show them all.

A short time later, Arun returned with a somewhat surly looking private. And how he was still a private, Tommy could only guess. The man had to be forty years old.

He came to attention, well, nearly attention, in front of Maurice. 'Ye wished to see me, Leftent Sar?' Maurice shook his head and then nodded to Tommy.

'No, my dear man, but he did.'

The man turned toward Tommy and looked him up and down, then raised his eyebrows.

'That's a lovely guitar mate, where'd you get it?' It wasn't lovely looking at all; it looked as if it was ready to fall apart.

'Snot stolen, if what ye's thinkin. My old Granpa took it off a dead Frenchie officer when we wuz fightin old Bony, an' its past to me down the lines so's ter speak.'

'Can I borrow it for a bit? I'll look after it, I promise,' Tommy said with a smile, though the soldier still looked dubious. 'Tell you what, me old mate, you lend me your guitar and you can have this.' He passed him what was left of the pork and bread.

The soldier's eyes widened and he nodded quickly, taking the food and passing the guitar in the same instant. The food disappeared into his dirty tunic and he went off down the incline. 'I be back fer it on the morn,' he said, and disappeared into the night.

Tommy turned to Arun. 'Can you pass me the lamp from inside the tent, please, mate.'

'Yes please, Sahib.' Thirty seconds later the lamp was on the table and Tommy was inspecting the guitar. Its neck was at an acute angle and the head was a funny rounded shape; he had no idea what the strings were made of and the saddle bridge looked broken. He strummed it to see if it was in tune. It sounded like a cat.

'Well, this looks promising, I must say. I'm so glad we – sorry, you – gave our breakfast away. I can't wait to hear it. Tell me, what time do the rest of the orchestra get here? I might start selling tickets, what.'

Tommy ignored him and continued playing with the keys whilst plucking the strings. Arun sat on the floor humming and bobbing his head as though this was the main show.

As he was tuning, he spoke to Maurice. 'When I was quite young, my old lady sent me to guitar practice. Hated it at first, until I was old enough to realise that girls love musicians. When I was a teenager, I started a band with my mates. Called ourselves Four Minute Warning. Crap, eh? It was a right laugh, though, and I honestly thought we were gonna be massive.'

'Well, that's all very well, Thomas, but could you do something, because Arun's humming is starting to grate.'

'Right, what would you like? I can do rock, jazz, anything. What do want? Actually, you know what, I don't think rock or jazz will be up your street. Luckily, though, I trained in classic.' And with that, he started to pluck the strings.

'This is "Capricho Arabe" by Tarrega,' said Tommy, as a tune started to emanate from the body of the guitar. 'This is one of the first pieces I tried to master when I was a kid, before I wanted to become a rock star, that is.'

As the classic guitar piece went on, so Maurice's mouth got wider. The sound was beautiful; not note-perfect because the guitar had seen better days, but still beautiful. The tune flowed out as Tommy's fingers flicked and plucked up and down the frets.

Arun had stopped humming and sat perfectly still, staring at the guitar as though it were alive. Maurice too had assumed the look of a sculpture. As the piece was coming to an end, Arun adopted a stupid, docile look.

Tommy finished. He leaned over and picked up his drink, took a sip and looked up at Maurice. There was a single tear running down his right cheek and an unbelievable look of sorrow on his face.

'Maurice, are you all right, mate?' asked Tommy, concerned.

'That was wonderful.'

'Cheers, pal,' he said. 'Do you wanna hear another one? Err, let's see, ah, got one. It's a bit quicker, this one, so I might make a few mistakes.' He started again. 'This is "Asturias". I can't remember who it's by, though.'

Tommy had to use all his concentration, as he hadn't played this piece for years, and he had to ad-lib a little, but seeing that they would never have heard it, he thought, *What the hell.*

His fingers were a blur, up and down the neck again, and as he was playing, he didn't notice Major Preston slide up out of the night and stand just behind the gawping Arun. He was soon joined by Captains Garratt and McMath, who also stood in amazement at the tune Tommy was creating.

He finished again and reached for his glass.

'Well, you are full of surprises, are you not, Mr Evans.'

Tommy choked on his mouthful of scotch and jumped to his feet, coughing. He stood to attention.

'I apologise for making you jump. Please, remain seated.'

'Major Preston, sir, would you care for a tipple? And who have you there in the shadows? Ah, Ernest, William, a pleasant evening to you both,' intoned Maurice smoothly.

'Well, it seems to me that you have been having the better evening listening to this fine musician. That was a fair bit of playing, sir, if I do say so myself.' The Captain walked forward and held out his hand; Tommy stood and grasped it. 'Captain William McMath, and this fellow officer is Captain Ernest Garratt.' The man who was clearly an Irishman stood aside to let Garratt shake Tommy's hand.

'Private Thomas Evans,' said Tommy formally.

'Well, don't let us ruin your playing. Please continue,' said Garratt.

'Would you look, Ernest, on the table. A bottle of whisky, by the looks of it,' said McMath with a smile.

'Sit, gentleman. I shall have Arun fetch us three more chairs,' chimed Maurice. 'Major, that drink?'

'I won't, thank you. The dinner with the General has sapped my strength somewhat, so I shall retire, a good evening to you gentlemen.' And Preston once again melted off into the night.

Arun returned with two more chairs and the Captains sat with a smile, while McMath produced two tumblers.

'So, Thomas,' said Garratt. 'You have a skill with that instrument. Tell me where you learnt it so well.'

Tommy glanced at Maurice, looking for some intervention, but none was forthcoming. 'My local vicar taught me, sir, from an early age. I picked it up quite fast. I seemed to have an ear for it.'

'Would you know any Irish tunes, Mr Evans?' asked McMath.

'Err.'

'Anything at all?'

'Well, all right, it's called "Sligo Creek". You probably won't know it. It's just something I picked up years ago.'

McMath nodded and sipped his drink.

Tommy played and the tune had all three officers tapping their feet to the fast Irish melody. As the three had been enthusiastic with that piece, Tommy decided to play more, using his best DADGAD, the famed Celtic method of guitar tuning, and he plucked away into the night. What neither Tommy nor the others realised, though, was that a crowd had gathered while he was playing, just out of the lamp light, in the shadows. And along with some tears of yearning for home, there were also a lot more feet tapping away to the music.

Later that evening, after they had retired to the hospital tent and the others back to theirs, Tommy lay on his bed listening to Maurice's light snoring, and thinking about his predicament. Why was he here? What was it for? Could he actually be in some sort of coma? Was he lying in a hospital bed somewhere with severe head wounds, surrounded by his family and friends? Is this what actually happened to those unfortunate people? They lose one life and then live in another, dreamlike one? Why this life though? If he'd had to choose a dream life, it wouldn't have been here, that's for sure. Maybe with his mates in a rock band or something like that. He would never have given the Victorian period a second thought, unless you don't get a choice. Maybe you just get dumped anywhere.

'Well, thank God it wasn't in the Roman times or something,' he muttered out loud. He would probably be dead by now… again…sort of.

Maurice mumbled in his sleep, 'Oh, that would be wonderful, Jane, my dear, but lock the door first. Saucy minx.'

Tommy smiled at his friend. Funny that, friend! An upper-class toff. But he was his friend, his only friend, actually. Tommy rolled onto his side and went to sleep.

The next day, after he had eaten some stew for breakfast, Tommy decided on another stroll.

'You want to have a look at those cannons, Maurice, or stay with Jane?'

'Bugger off.'

Tommy smiled. It seemed Maurice genuinely couldn't handle his drink one bit; he huffed and rolled over away from Tommy.

'Suit yourself, mate, but I wanna take a quick butcher's.' He put his uniform on; he had gotten the hang of it by now and decided he needed to get it washed because it was filthy. Maybe Arun would do it? The wallah had been hero-worshipping Tommy since he had watched him play that old guitar. He caught a scent of something and sniffed under his arm.

'Christ! I smell like a dead dog or something. Oh, for a can of deodorant.' He stopped getting dressed. 'Right,' he said to himself, 'I am gonna have a wash,' and he took off his tunic. He walked out of the tent into the mid-morning sunshine and searched for Arun, who was squatting by a large cooking pot.

'Arun, me old mate, do us a favour. Can you wash my uniform, please? It stinks.'

The wallah jumped up. 'Yes please, Private Sahib, right away Private Sahib, yes please.'

'And I don't suppose you could manage some water and some shower gel – sorry, soap – could you?'

'Yes please, Private Sahib.' And with that he turned and disappeared round the back of a cart that was parked next to the hospital tent. A few minutes later he returned with a large bucket of water and placed it in front of Tommy. 'Will Private Sahib be wanting a shaving also?'

Tommy rubbed his chin and found at least a week's growth. 'Sure, why not.' Arun still stood in front of Tommy with a confused look. 'Yes please, mate.'

Arun gave a big toothy smile. 'Jolly good, Private Sahib,' he said, and produced from nowhere a cut-throat razor.

Tommy jumped. 'Shit!'

'For chin, for chin, Private Sahib.' Tommy had been expecting a Bic razor for some reason. Arun indicated for Tommy to sit on a stool he had dragged over from outside the tent; he then started to rub a little round brush into a big block of something that Tommy presumed was soap, which he dipped it into the bucket every now and then. Once he had worked up quite a good lather, he said, 'Please be opening shirt, Private Sahib.'

Tommy reached for the shirt laces at his neck but then decided to take the thing off, so he pulled the whole garment over his head. Tommy was proud of his body; he worked out in the gym as much as possible, when he could get in there, of course, so he was quite well muscled in an athletic sort of way. He also had a fair share of tattoos, and this was what made Arun stop what he was doing and stare in fascination.

'Do you like them, Arun?' Tommy asked when he noticed the other man staring.

'Private Sahib, you are having beautiful paintings all over body.'

'They're tattoos, me old mate, not paintings, and they cost me a fortune.' He paused, then: 'Watch.' He grabbed the rough flannel from the bucket and rubbed at the Celtic cross on the top of his right arm. 'You see? You can't wash them off.'

Arun leaned down and traced his finger over the tattoo on Tommy's right bicep. 'This is being your tribe, Private Sahib? Your army?'

'No, mate,' Tommy chuckled, 'that's a football team. Man United, the Red Army.'

'Ah, I am knowing football, Private Sahib. Robert Vidal, the Wanderer, a truly great man, yes please.'

'Err, yeah, I suppose so, mate.' Tommy had no idea what he was on about. He sat on the stool and waited as Arun lathered his face. He gave him the closest shave Tommy had ever had. After rinsing off with some water and then wiping his face with a towel, he asked Arun if he had a mirror, as he realised he hadn't seen his own face in a while. Arun disappeared for a few moments and then returned with a small ornately carved wooden box about the size of a house brick. He lifted the lid and handed it to Tommy, who hesitated. He had the awful notion that the face in the mirror wouldn't be his own. He hesitantly took the box and gazed into the mirror, and to his relief the face looking back was indeed his own. Tommy inspected his face closely and he noticed a few light bruises, but they were yellowing, nearly healed. He had a slightly black left eye as well, but apart from that, he looked relatively well, maybe just a little thinner in the face, though not surprising, with the crap they ate here.

'Thanks, Arun, that's got to be the best shave I've ever had, mate.'

Arun bobbed his head up and down. 'Yes please, Private Sahib,' he said, and handed Tommy the large block of soap. Tommy took it and, leaning over the bucket, he began to wash. The soap was efficient but bloody awful to use, and the scent was a strong chemical one as opposed to the perfumed version he was used to. *Oh well, it is quite invigorating*, he thought.

Twenty or so minutes later he, was drying himself off with a rough flannel; he had also washed his short hair, cut military-style, which had also been filthy. After looking in the little mirror, he was pleased to see his natural brown colour was back, and not the greasy, dirty thing that had greeted him before he had washed it.

Arun approached him. 'Pardons Private Sahib, I have cleaned tunic.'

Tommy accepted the dry uniform and, realising a vigorous brushing was all he was going to get, he put it on. Now smelling a bit better, well, more than his pet dog's basket anyway, he thanked Arun and strolled off into the camp, making his way over towards the cannon he had seen yesterday. Or the day before. His body clock was totally off, he realised. In fact, it already felt like years since he was on patrol with Jacko and had gotten hit with that RPG, and entered Narnia.

He approached the row of cannons and was amazed to find how new they looked. *Idiot! Of course they're new*, he thought, *or newish, anyway.* The last cannon he had seen had been hundreds of years old and kept in a castle back home. As Tommy got a little closer, he noticed some native mud-built houses beyond the guns. *A village*, he thought, realising that he hadn't noticed them before now. That made him wonder where exactly he was.

Just before he reached the nearest cannon, 'Can I help you, Private?' came a strong but quiet voice.

Tommy turned and saw an officer walking toward him. Realising the role he had to play, he came to attention.

'Pardon me, Sir. I wus just admiring the cannons, sir,' he said in the best cockney accent he could muster, remembering Jacko with fondness.

'Are you, by God. Well why don't you stop playing at infantryman and join the Royal Horse Artillery then, eh? Become a galloping gunner?' He said this with a stern, clipped voice, but also with a slight smile.

Tommy hesitated.

'At ease, Private. So, what do you make of our little toys, then?'

'They're beautiful, sir,' replied Tommy.

The officer smiled. 'That they are, Private,' he said, but before he could continue, another soldier trotted up and came to attention.

'Captain Slade, sir,' he panted, 'Major Blackwood sends his compliments and asks that you join him and the rest of the officers in his tent in ten minutes.'

The Captain became thoughtful for a moment. He inhaled deeply through the nose and nodded to himself. 'So it begins,' he said quietly. He looked over at Tommy, 'My apologies, Private. Sorry, you didn't tell me your name.'

'Thomas Evans of the 66th Foot, sir.'

'Well, Private Thomas Evans of the 66th Foot, I must leave you, but feel free to ask Gunner Bale here any questions you might have. Farewell.'

The Captain walked off into the mass of tents and Tommy was left with the bemused Gunner Bale.

'What questions have do you have, then?' asked Bale.

'None really, mate. I was just looking at the cannon when the Captain came over. Just admiring, really.'

Bale frowned. 'Mate? Anyhow, these are muzzle-loading nine pounders. They fire case shot, explosive and shrapnel. Has that answered your questions, Evans?'

'My name's Thomas, or Tommy if you like.'

Bale smiled. 'My name happens to be Thomas as well. Pleased to meet yer,' he said, and held out his hand, which Tommy shook.

Bale smiled. 'I have a few minutes to spare if yer like, to tell yer about the guns, but it'll have to be quick mind, else Sergeant Mullane will give me a roasting!'

Tommy nodded.

'Well, like's I said, these here are nine pounder rifled barrels, but we also got some smooth bore, a couple of Howitzers and the rest are field guns – we took these off those levies.'

Tommy was genuinely interested and was about to ask about shells when he heard a commotion behind one of the tents where the Grenadiers were: raised voices and the sound of pots and pans tipping over.

Just then Arun came sprinting round the corner of a tent and nearly collided with Gunner Bale. 'Hey, watch where yer running, you bloody heathen!' he shouted.

Tommy reached out and grabbed Arun's arm, bringing him to a standstill. 'Arun, what's up, mate?' Tommy asked, concerned with the look of fear on his face.

Arun stopped panicking when he saw it was Tommy. 'Pardons, Private Sahib, but I am making message for Major Preston Sahib with the request for having more tents from baggage. But I having trouble on the way with giant soldier of Grenadier for trying to help old chai wallah.'

He said all this quite breathlessly and was visibly shaking.

'Show me,' said Tommy. But Arun quickly shook his head and his eyes nearly popped out.

'Everything will be alright, Arun, I'll be with you. Thomas, good luck, mate,' he said, turning to Gunner Bale and shaking his hand again.

Bale shrugged. 'Aye, you too, Tommy lad,' he said, and with that he turned and walked away.

Reluctantly, Arun led Tommy to where he had heard the noises, and as he rounded the nearest tent, Tommy had a flash back of memory.

It was the scene all over again, but instead of Sergeant Adams standing over an old man, it was the nasty looking Grenadier boxer standing over a terrified Bhisti wallah. As Tommy and

Arun neared, the Grenadier slapped the wallah across the face and shouted something at him.

Arun quailed back, but Tommy stepped up and stood in front of the wallah as he had done with the old man. The Grenadier had about three inches on him, so Tommy had to look up. And what he saw looking back was contempt.

'Why don't ya pick on someone your own size, mate?'

The Grenadier chuckled with a deep, throaty sound, and Tommy could now see his face. It was scarred; a white line stood out against his brown skin and ran from his forehead above his left eye, straight down to his bearded top lip. His left eye was unusually pale in comparison to the other bright blue one, and when this guy smiled at him, Tommy saw quite a few missing teeth.

This fella, Tommy realised, was the stuff of nightmares.

A few other Grenadiers had gathered round and one of them was talking in a language he later found out was Hindi. The Grenadier replied to his comrade in a voice laced with humour. His friend nodded and turned to Tommy, 'Naik Singh wishes you to please be moving, Private of Infantry, so he can finish his business with the wallah who burnt him with tea.'

Tommy was taken back once again to the Arsehole and the old bearded man. He looked down at the wallah, who was gazing back with the same fear in his face as the young Afghan who had been knocked about by Dinga. Tommy could feel the anger building, a buzzing sensation that started in his fingertips and made his ears ring. He looked back at the hulking man in front of him.

'I don't think so, me old mate, not today. So why don't you piss off!'

The interpreter jabbered again in Hindi and the smile dropped off Singh's face. He leaned down a little, stared at Tommy with his one clear eye and started jabbering again.

'The Naik is saying you will move, little Englishman, or he will be moving you.'

A crowd had gathered at this point.

Tommy slid his right foot back so he was more side-on, and lowered his forehead; he assumed a solid fighting stance, the one he was taught by his kick-boxing instructor for many years.

'You can tell this dickhead,' said Tommy, who's voice was rising along with his anger, 'that if he wants some, I'm right here.'

Singh looked as if he was about to strike Tommy when a loud voice sounded above the now-swelling crowd of Grenadiers, 66th and some of the Gunners.

'ENOUGH.'

The crowd parted and an officer walked through, followed by a large sergeant.

They crowd fell silent and the Grenadier, as well as Tommy, came to attention.

'Would somebody like to tell me what the devil is going on here? Well?'

A sergeant of the Grenadiers stepped forward. 'Lieutenant Sahib, this Private of Infantry attempted to stop my Naik going about his business and was behaving aggressively.'

The officer looked at Tommy.

'Is this correct, Private?'

Tommy didn't speak for a moment.

'I ask you again, Private, were you aggressive towards this Corporal going about his duties? Need I remind you that a strike or even an attempted one on a superior is punishable by death?'

Tommy looked straight into the man's eyes. 'Sir, this Grenadier was beating a wallah for no other reason than accidently spilling hot tea on him, sir.'

The officer looked over at Singh and did a double-take. He became thoughtful for a moment. 'Did you beat a wallah, Corporal, for this reason?'

'Yes sir, Lieutenant Sahib,' although he answered; he did not look at the officer but stared into the distance.

Tommy looked for the wallah but he had cleared off. The officer was silent for a moment.

'So how are we supposed to remedy this situation, then, Private, eh? Do you have any suggestions?' He stepped closer to Tommy so that only he could hear. 'Now don't go upsetting the native soldiers, Private. They already assume that we think they are inferior, including that brute. Do you think you could have handled him had I not intervened?' He said this with a twinkle in his eye.

Tommy caught on. 'Yes sir, I propose a boxing match, sir.'

'A boxing match, you say?'

'Yes sir, but a match that incorporates other fighting skills as well as boxing, sir.'

'Do you, by God. Well, what say you to that, Corporal? Would you accept a fight from the Private here?'

Singh looked Tommy up and down and smiled. 'Yes, Lieutenant Sahib,' he said.

The officer nodded.

'Well then, I propose that we meet in, say, one hour at the Grenadiers' camp. And I will be refereeing the match. Does that suit you both?'

They both nodded their agreement.

'Good. Dismissed.' The Grenadiers moved off, with them all laughing and patting Singh on the back.

Tommy made to move off but a voice called him back.

'Hold,' said the officer, and he moved in close to Tommy. 'Are you mad, Private?' he whispered. 'Do you honestly think you can win against that brute?'

'Well, we'll have to wait and see, sir.'

'I watched that man beat to a pulp the 66th champion, and I hear he knows that Sikh style of unarmed combat. I do believe you've bitten off a tad more than you can chew.'

Tommy shrugged.

'I did lose money on Davis, but you seem awfully confident. Very well, then. Dismissed.'

Tommy turned, and as he started to make his way back to Preston's tent, found Arun hiding behind a cart.

'C'mon mate, let's get a cup of chai, shall we?' But Arun stopped in front of him.

'Please do not be fighting Grenadier. Private Sahib, that soldier is animal, you will be being hurt, yes please,' he pleaded with Tommy, all the way back to the tent.

'You've done what?' blustered Maurice. 'Have you utterly lost your wits?'

Tommy was sipping the tea that Arun had brought him, and he smiled back at his friend.

'I don't believe this. It's too ridiculous to contemplate. Did you not have eyes in that thick skull of yours yesterday? Did you not observe that goliath make our champion look like… like…I don't know, a woman! For heaven's sake, Thomas, you're going to get killed or badly injured at least, all for the sake of a bloody chai wallah!'

'I couldn't give a shit who it was for, Maurice, a wallah or the Queen. I hate bullies!'

'Do you honestly believe you stand a chance against that man? He will tear you apart, Thomas, he is a beast, an animal, a creature of hell. Well he looks like one, anyway, but what I'm trying to elucidate to you is that, well, I don't want you to get hurt, old chap.'

'Thanks for the show of confidence.'

'It's not about confidence, my friend, it's about intelligence. Why do you want to put yourself in harm's way for such an asinine notion?'

'What the bloody hell is this army out here for, then? Since we're talking about being in harm's way…and Maurice, why the hell have you attached yourself to it if you want to stay safe? I couldn't think of a worse position or place to be in.'

Tommy stood up and looked at his friend with a new warmth. 'Tell you what, me old pal, how about you just wish me luck, eh?' He turned and walked to the tent entrance.

'Wait, wait, I'm coming with you.' Maurice threw his helmet and tunic on and began to button it as he followed Tommy.

They made their way down towards the already forming ring, and Tommy was surprised to find quite a large crowd had formed. There were different uniforms everywhere, and as he got closer, Tommy could see the amount of money changing hands. *Well, well, what do you know*, thought Tommy.

'Maurice, have you got any cash, mate?'

'A gentleman does not carry spare change, Thomas, it's not the done thing. But if you're thinking what I'm thinking, my word is good.'

'Well, why don't you put a few quid on me to win?'

Maurice looked at him in surprise, 'A few quid? You do mean shillings, don't you?'

'Eh, what you on about? Pounds, Maurice, you know, sterling.'

'That's an exceptionally large amount, old chap. If you were to fail, well, that's a lot of money, Thomas.'

'Just do it, mate.'

Tommy took off his tunic and then his shirt. His tattoos drew a lot of curious glances, including the officer from earlier, who was making his way across the square toward him.

'My dear Thomas, how the devil are you?' said Maurice. 'What brings you into the ranks of the unwashed masses?'

'Hello Maurice. Well, I am here in an official capacity, actually. I am the referee for this fight between,' he looked at Tommy, 'this young man here and that enormous mountain of terror over there,' he said, indicating Corporal Singh, who had just made his way into the square.

'Have you been introduced? No? Well, may I present Private Thomas Evans of the 66th Foot. Thomas, may I introduce Lieutenant Thomas Henn, an Engineer with the Bombay Sappers and Miners.'

Tommy nodded. 'We've already met, Maurice,' he said, and he put on the gloves that were supplied by a smiling Grenadier.

Henn gave Tommy a strange look and wondered as to the familiarity between these two, but shook his head and sniffed, 'Yes, Maurice, we have indeed. In fact, I was trying to encourage the young man not to trade punches with that monster. Did you see what he did to that poor private from your regiment? Poor chap still can't see properly, so I've heard.' He sniffed again and looked hurt. 'I lost 10 shillings on the oaf!'

Henn looked over to the Grenadiers' corner. 'Well, it looks as though the Grenadier is ready. Shall we begin?' He walked off toward the centre of the square.

While Henn had been talking, Tommy had been stretching his muscles and controlling his breathing, and was now ready. He took a last look at Maurice, who was sporting a horrified expression, and rubbed his forefinger and thumb together, mouthing the word, 'Money!'

Tommy strolled up to Henn and the expressionless Grenadier. He stretched his neck muscles and jumped up and down on the spot.

Henn gave Tommy a funny look and shrugged. 'Right, gentlemen, seeing that this is a mixed-fighting-art thingy,' he shrugged again, 'all I have to say is, well, good luck.' And with that, he moved backward, put his hand out and shouted, 'Begin!'

Tommy sprang backwards as a left jab snaked out from Singh and caught fresh air. Tommy smiled at him and slowly moved around the square. The Indian turned in the centre, watching him, expressionless.

'What's the matter, dickhead? A bit quicker than the last one, eh?'

With a sudden lunge that surprised Tommy, Singh shot forward and, crouching down, attempted to grab him around the waist; Tommy shifted sideways and slapped the top of his head, surprised at how easy this was. But, as he caught him, Singh's left hand flew out and caught Tommy's ankle. Before he knew what was happening, he was on his back and scrambling backwards through the dust with Singh bearing down on him. He flipped over and sprang to his feet just before Singh could grab him. Tommy trotted away and sized up his opponent again. *So that's your game*, he thought, *get in close, wrestle me down and use that superior strength.*

Tommy carried on backing away, thinking, while Singh followed slowly, smiling now. The crowd had started to jeer, but Tommy ignored them. He knew his business and this guy was dangerous. He had changed tactics, and although he was good with his fists, he had favoured another method and that made Tommy wary. As he passed by his own corner, he noticed Maurice talking to one of the moneylenders. *What a backstabber*, he thought. *He thinks I'm gonna lose!* Singh stepped forward a few paces, and looked as if he was going to lunge again. *Fuck it!* thought Tommy, *Bring it on*. And he braced himself.

The crowd was roaring, but it was such a noise that no particular voice could be heard. Tommy had reached a sense of calmness now and didn't move as the Grenadier came forward another step. He positioned himself in a classic Taekwondo fighting stance. With another lightning lunge, Singh launched himself at Tommy's midriff, but this time Tommy was expecting the low manoeuvre. When Singh was just feet away, Tommy performed a perfect roundhouse kick that took the other man in the side of the head. As the Grenadier staggered sideways, Tommy spun on the spot and landed back in the fighting stance. But he did not follow up.

'That's right, I am gonna make you suffer, you knobhead,' he said, and smiled at the now-frowning Grenadier.

'STOP.'

The booming voice of Henn resounded around the square, and he trotted up in between the fighters.

'Back to your corners. End of the round, gentlemen,' he said, and he put his arms out, palms up, to emphasise this. Time had flown by as the two fighters had circled each other. Tommy walked backwards to his corner remembering that last punch that Singh had used on the 66th champion. *Well*, he thought, *you're not catching me out, me old mate*. The Grenadier glared as he made his way back.

'My God, Thomas, where did you learn to move like that?' said Maurice. 'That was incredible.'

'Yeah, well, it's not over yet, Maurice.'

'Thomas, I think you should know that Burrows is here with his staff.'

Tommy looked at his friend with a little confusion, 'Sorry, who?'

'The General of our little party, our glorious leader, El Cid!'

'Oh, right, nice. But I've got bigger things to worry about, mucka, like that big twat over there.'

Henn's voice sounded again, 'Right, gentlemen, ready?'

Tommy shook out his arms and hopped on the spot. *Right, you ugly fucker*, he thought, *let's have it*. He walked to the centre again and eyed up the Grenadier, who had, this time, an angry look on his face. *Oh dear*, thought Tommy, *you look a little peeved! Let's see what we can make of that, shall we*.

'Begin!' shouted Henn. Both fighters stepped back, now wary of their opponent; they slowly started to circle each other. It was getting late in the afternoon and Tommy was starting to feel the heat. He wiped at the sweat running down his face. Singh noticed this and smiled at Tommy. *Shit!* he thought, *If this goes on much longer I'll faint with the heat. It needs to be finished*.

The other man knew this as well, because he was quite content to keep walking round the square, tiring Tommy and waiting for his moment.

'Ok, mate, that's it,' said Tommy, and with that he stopped and assumed a fighting stance. The crowd were baying for blood, and it wasn't long in coming. The Indian stopped his pacing, moved towards Tommy with raised hands and nodded. *He wants to trade*, Tommy thought. *Alright then, mate*, and beckoned Singh forward with his hand. A split second later, a flurry of blows were thrown at Tommy's head, left jab, right cross, jab, hook, jab, cross, upper cut. It was all Tommy could do just to bob and weave and take some of the punches on his forearms. *Fuck me!* thought Tommy. *This guy is fast*.

Just as the last punch landed, Singh feigned a lunge for Tommy's lower body. Tommy sprang back, ready to counter a low attack, but the Indian lunged back upwards and landed a heavy blow to Tommy's unprotected forehead. It was a stunner and he flew back with the blow, though managed to stay on his feet. *Shit*, he thought, *that hurt*, and shuffled backwards as Singh came at him with a flurry of punches, elbow strikes and backhands. It was all Tommy could do just to block or dodge. They broke apart again and Tommy backed off a little, shook his head and tried to regain some composure. The Grenadier, meanwhile, was thumping his chest and shouting something in Hindi. Tommy caught his breath, silenced his doubts and, smiling, beckoned the Grenadier on.

He came at him again, this time trying a kick at his left knee, but Tommy just lifted his leg and took the blow, followed the motion through and countered with a twist, full circle, and landed a backhand into the other man's cheek. Singh staggered sideways and went down on one knee. Tommy was about to follow this up, but he noticed the Indian had grabbed a handful of sand and was going to throw it at his face. He turned at the last second, managing to dodge the dirt aimed for his eyes, and landed a fast left jab to Singh's jaw. This stunned the man enough for Tommy to follow up with a fast right cross, shattering the man's nose, and as he tumbled backward, Tommy scissor kicked him in the chest. The big Grenadier landed on his arse. But rather than stay down, he attempted to get to his feet, so Tommy leaned back and at the same time lifted his bent right leg, flicking it out with force and connecting with the other man's jaw. He was unconscious before he hit the ground.

The crowd were in an uproar, shouting and baying at the now-sleeping giant. Tommy staggered back to a delighted and clapping Maurice. 'Well done, well done, old chap. That was a most titillating performance.'

'You're sure about that? I saw you betting against me.'

'Betting against you, whatever for? I have the utmost faith in your abilities, Thomas. Always have. Now if you will excuse me, I will go and collect my winnings.' And with a flourish, he moved off through the still-roaring crowd.

Arun passed him his tunic and a drink of water, which he downed in one, and thanked the wallah who was now nearly on his knees in admiration. Tommy was aching badly and motioned for Arun to follow him back to the tent. When he got there, he collapsed onto his bed, absolutely drained. Between the heat and the giant Grenadier he felt exhausted, and the pain in his head had come back. 'What was I thinking?' he said, remembering that punch to the forehead.

'Does Private Sahib need anything else?'

104

'No thanks, mate. I think I'm gonna have a nap. Can you wake me in a couple of hours?' Without waiting for an answer, he closed his eyes and fell asleep. The wallah smiled for a few moments, looking down at the already-sleeping form.

'Sleep well, Thomas Evans Sahib,' he whispered, and left the tent.

Chapter 8

Orders

Tommy yawned, a real jaw-stretching, eye-watering, head-quivering yawn. He smacked his lips and looked blurrily around the tent. *I need a drink*, he thought, and sat up. *Oh shit!* The pain in his joints was killing him; he remembered the fight with the Grenadier Corporal and groaned outwardly. After a few moments of regretting ever getting involved, he swung his aching legs over the side of the bed and stood. There was a subdued light from outside and, with no lamp in the tent, it felt quite claustrophobic. *Out*, he thought to himself. Fresh air was what he needed, so he made his way to the entrance.

It was strangely quiet as he walked out into the dusk of the day. Well, not that quiet; there were the usual noises of life in a large camp, but something was amiss, something subdued, something not quite right. He looked for Maurice but couldn't see him or Major Preston. He even checked for the wallah. No one. No one near his tent, anyway. He sat at the little table and looked into the distance. *Strange*, he thought, *it seems as though the camp is holding its breath*. After ten minutes or so, Arun came toward the table from out of the darkness.

'Good evenings, Private Sahib. Are you wanting any refreshment?'

'Oh, yes please, mate, can I have a cup of chai, and if you have anything to eat, that would be great.'

'One moment, yes please,' he said, and he skipped off.

Tommy wondered where Maurice had got to and realised that he felt quite alone without his new friend. Although he spoke like a typical upper-class university-trained politician who had swallowed a dictionary, Tommy liked him; there was a warmness to him, a friendly openness and a ready smile. It was typical of the times, though, he thought, the way they treated people who they thought were of a lower class, but he supposed that was normal and shouldn't make too much of it. After all he, thought, it's already happened, maybe?

After about ten or fifteen minutes, Arun returned with a steaming mug of tea. It was black and unsweetened, but what the hell, Tommy thought, it was wet and hot. He also placed a lamp on the table so Tommy could see with the failing light, and as the lamp wick flickered, he produced another lovely bowl of meat slop. But Tommy was far too hungry to moan and dug in immediately. After he had finished, to his surprise and delight, Arun produced an apple out of his sleeve like a magician.

'Where the bloody hell did you get that, mate?'

'Private Sahib, I am keeping supply secrets, yes please.' He smiled at Tommy, picked up his empty bowl and went off to whatever secret place he gets his work done. Tommy had eaten better apples but this was a godsend after the tasteless food these soldiers ate. He would never again moan about the ration packs supplied to him, and he relished every juicy bite.

About an hour later, he was considering going back to bed when he heard Maurice's voice coming out of the darkness. A moment later he appeared, once again carrying a bottle of some sort of liquor.

'Yes please, Arun, and could you fetch a glass for Mr Evans also.'

'Yes please, Lieutenant Sahib.'

'Thomas, my dear chap, I have news.' He said this as he sat on the opposite chair and uncorked the bottle.

Arun returned a moment later with two glasses and handed them to the two soldiers.

'That will be all for tonight, my good man. Why don't you take the rest of the evening off, unless of course the Major Sahib requires your attendance.'

'Very good, Lieutenant Sahib, yes please.' Arun disappeared into the darkness.

Maurice poured two healthy measures into the glasses and re-corked the bottle; his hands, Tommy noticed, had a slight tremble. Maurice took a large gulp and turned to his friend.

'We should have our orders by tomorrow, Thomas, and we might be moving in the next couple of days.' He became silent.

Tommy took a generous swig of the scotch and tried to understand Maurice's mood but found he was hard to gauge. He watched him for a few more moments and then decided to press him for details. 'So what's the deal then, mate?'

Maurice was gazing over the now-dark camp, staring at the camp fires; he completely ignored Tommy. 'Maurice, what's the score then, me old mate?' he said, louder this time, which got Maurice's attention.

'Hmm, oh sorry, old chap,' he said absentmindedly.

'What's the deal, then? Where are we moving to exactly?'

'Sorry Thomas, I was miles away. Yes, well, the cavalry reports say that they have made contact with Ayub Khan's forward screen and his army has fully crossed the Helmand. And Burrows believes they will be making for, or bypassing, Kandahar and heading for Kabul, so he has decided to intercept and stop them. Shouldn't be too much of a problem, he says. The enemy have about six thousand men and around four thousand cavalry, and there are also reports of around thirty guns.' Maurice stopped and took a drink.

Tommy frowned. 'How many men do we have, then?'

'Well, there are around three thousand of the force that left Kandahar; a mix of infantry, us, of course, the 66th; the 130th Jacob's Rifles; the 1st Grenadiers, who you have already met, of course; two regiments of cavalry, the Bombay Light and the 3rd Sind.' He paused and took a sip of his drink. 'We also have the guns of the Royal Horse and the smooth bore we captured, which are now attached to the 66th, plus the sappers and miners, of course. More than enough for those heathens, the Brigadier General assures us.'

Tommy was thoughtful for a moment as he sipped his drink; something was nagging him, a memory he could not quite put his finger on. Try though he might, he just couldn't remember what was niggling him.

'You are particularly thoughtful, Thomas. Something troubles you?'

'What? Oh, sorry, I was just thinking about what you just said. I seem to remember something…well, I don't actually remember, that is, but I feel I have to remember, if you know what I mean?'

Maurice shook his head and smiled. 'Thomas, my dear chap, you really are a heteroclite individual.'

'Well, whatever that means, thanks. Sorry mate, it's just, I don't know, something's not right. I have a right shitty feeling about all of this now.' He stood and walked to the edge of the lamp light and stood, thoughtful, watching the light from the fires. *What? What is it? What the hell is bothering me so much?* he thought. *Why is this information affecting me so much?* Then he remembered about his journey on the cart, what that bloke had said. *What was his name now? Watson! Yes, that was it. Now what did he say?* But Tommy still couldn't figure it out, so went back to the table.

When he sat, he noticed Maurice had consumed more of the liquor and was pouring himself yet another. *He wasn't right*, Tommy thought. He had become a little pale and he had a faraway look in his eyes. Then a thought came to him.

'Maurice, where are we due to meet this enemy, what was his name again?'

'Ayub Khan.'

'Right, and where is this fella supposed to be when the brigade intercepts him?'

'Oh, not too far. We will hopefully meet him at or somewhere near a place called Maiwand.'

Tommy went cold and placed his glass on the table with a bump. The memory came back to him with a rush, and that niggling thought he couldn't remember washed over him like a tidal wave. The history lesson in school about the battle of Maiwand. Now he remembered. The different regiments, the

66th, of course. Watson was right. Tommy had thought the battle had been near Kabul but it hadn't been, had it? It was bloody Kandahar!

With a sudden sense of realisation and then cold, stark dread, he picked up his glass and downed the fiery contents in one. He ran a hand through his hair.

'Fucking hell,' he said, with a slightly lighter voice.

'I say, you look rather pale, old chap,' smiled Maurice. He looked at the drawn look on Tommy's face and the smile faded. 'What is the matter, Thomas?'

Tommy just reached for the bottle and poured himself another, and downed that in one. He was mumbling to himself, which was starting to unsettle Maurice.

'Thomas, I don't care for the theatrics. If you have something to say, then bloody well say it, and stop drinking all the scotch!'

'Maurice, what is the date today?'

'Oh for heaven's sake, Tho—'

'What's the date, you arsehole?' he butted in.

Maurice went quiet, mouth agape. 'How dare you speak to me that way,' he said quietly. 'Try to remember, Thomas, even though we are friends I am still your superior officer.'

'All right, I'm sorry, but could you please tell me the date?' Tommy was now becoming extremely agitated.

'It is the twenty-sixth day of July,' Maurice pouted.

'The year?'

Maurice sighed heavily. 'Well, if you must keep up this charade, it is 1880. Now, could you please explain why you are doing a rather good, and frightening, I might say, impression of an absolute lunatic?'

Tommy was feeling the most helpless he had ever felt in his life. Even if he was asleep or in a coma, the bombshell that Maurice had just dropped on him took his breath away. Is this it? Is this the reason why he was here? But why? To do what?

'Maurice,' Tommy looked squarely at his friend, 'if this brigade meets those Afghans tomorrow, it will be destroyed.'

Maurice sat nursing his drink with a bemused look on his face. After a few moments, he said, 'Thomas, honestly, you worry too much. This is the British Army, for goodness sake. Disciplined troops, well-armed, professional soldiers against a few thousand heathen tribesmen. What an unbelievably silly notion.'

'Maurice, it's true. I know you think I've lost the plot, but I remember this from school. They were a few thousand troops when they started out, but they were joined by thousands of Ghazis, *thousands*, Maurice. They joined Ayub Khan on his march. And their guns, yes, I remember now! Their guns, Maurice, they were modern pieces, breech loaders I think, and it was said they were manned by some Russian gunners. Shit! It's all coming back to me now.'

Maurice sighed and tried to look sceptical, but the colour had drained from his face as he poured himself another drink. After all, this common soldier sitting in front of him had proved on more than one occasion that there was nothing common about him at all. He was starting to feel the effects of the scotch now and a host of nasty thoughts were going through his head. *What if? No! That's a preposterous thought, ridiculous, very Jules Verne, in fact.*

He smiled at Tommy. 'Come, Thomas, have another drink and forget these silly ideas.'

'Their cannons will out-gun ours and will create havoc. Our own will run out of ammo and withdraw. I can't remember at what point that was, but it's a turning point in the battle. The Jacob's Rifles will fold under the pressure; they were untested, apparently, and they will bend and fall into the Grenadiers' rear, which will have already lost something like a third, or even half, I don't recall the numbers.' Tommy was recounting the history books now, and he was saying all this whilst looking straight through Maurice with a clouded expression.

Maurice had assumed a horrified look and was visibly shaking. The things Tommy was saying were terrifying, and for a moment he thought he was actually listening to the Devil himself.

'The Grenadiers will collapse onto the rear of the 66th, then all will be lost. It will be every man for himself. The ones who stay with the colours will die to the last man.'

'*Enough*.' Maurice stood, indignant. 'How dare you say such things, even in jest. We are on the eve of battle.' He took a deep breath and looked around to make sure no one was listening. 'I tell you this, Thomas, if I were someone else, you would be whipped for saying such cowardly things.'

Tommy stood with hands outstretched towards his friend. 'I'm so sorry, Maurice, but that's what's going to happen. Our army's finished, and by tomorrow night, what's left of it will be in a full, horrific and desperate retreat back to Kandahar.'

Maurice sat and poured some more of his scotch. 'Even though you tell a vivid tale, Thomas, and make it sound so true, in the end a tale it is.' He paused. 'But tell me, are you thinking of stealing off in the night?'

'Where would I go, Maurice? No, I'm hoping I will wake up out of this nightmare. If you have any family, you might want to write them a letter and leave it with certain higher ranking officers. I'll try and remember the ones who survive and you can ask them to post it back home to whatever country estate it is you live on.'

Tommy sat. He didn't have to worry about it, did he, as he was already dead, or asleep or something, so this didn't affect him one bit. He looked over at Maurice, who had now fallen silent, a glum look on his face. Tommy felt for his friend.

A notion came to mind, then, a brilliant notion. *What*, he thought, *if I'm here to save Maurice? What*, he thought, *if I'm here to save the Army?*

'I don't live on a country estate.'

'Sorry mate, you don't what?'

'I don't live on a country estate, Thomas,' Maurice replied in a sad voice.

'Oh, I thought you might have been the son of a lord or something. You sound like one, anyway, with all the fancy words.'

Maurice looked at Tommy with a sad smile. 'My father was a Liverpool merchant, a successful one, I grant you, but a merchant all the same. I was sent away and educated at Temple Grove School under Master Waterfield, alias The Cow.

Brilliant at teaching, even better at a good beating.' He took another sip of his drink and Tommy realised Maurice badly wanted to talk about this.

'I then went to Harrow for a time, until I left to take my army examination. I passed sixty-fifth out of three hundred odd candidates to get my army appointment, which I got with the 66th. I was not given everything on a platter, Thomas, as you presume. I took steady beatings from The Cow, I read, I threw myself into sports − cricket mainly − I read some more and decided, a merchant's second son or no, nobody will look down on me.' He paused and looked Tommy straight in the eyes. 'So now you know why I prefer to use gargantuan, beclouding confabulation. It confuses the officers who are boors and have gained entry into the army not on merit, but by status.'

They both sat quietly for a time, sipping drinks and watching the camp. After a while, Maurice piped up. 'Besides, Thomas, we might not get any orders at all within the next couple of days, so that will put pay to your turn of events, will it not?'

'Maurice, if the date today is 26 July 1880, the orders will be given about half ten tonight. What time is it now, by the way?'

Maurice looked at his pocket watch. 'It is fifteen minutes past the hour of nine.' He looked at Tommy with uncertainty. 'Well, I suppose we won't have to wait very long.'

He poured some more of the scotch into both their glasses, and for the next hour they talked about Maurice's background and more about his school days, which he compared with Tommy's. He was shocked to learn of the education Tommy had received, how there were just as many women teachers as masters, though they weren't called that anymore, and he was particularly shocked at the now redundant use of the cane.

'Well, how do you punish your youngsters?' he had asked.

'We keep them behind after school doing extra work, or we take their mobiles or iPods or whatever else they have sneaked into school.'

Maurice fell silent again, staring into his glass. Tommy watched him with pity, knowing that quite a few officers of the 66th died at the battle. And he was hoping that Maurice wasn't one of them.

After some time sitting in silence, an officer walked up out of the darkness and approached Maurice.

'Chute, old chap, what brings you here on this wonderful evening? Would you like a drink?' Maurice greeted.

'Hello Rayner. Well, I'm here in an official capacity, actually. Galbraith sends his compliments and asks if you are quite recovered, as he has need of you and wonders if you would attend him as soon as you may. And I will accept that drink, thank you.'

After Maurice had given up his chair and supplied him with his own glass, the man Chute sat, raised the glass in a quick salute and downed it in one. After a moment he seemed to notice Tommy, who was idly staring at him with interest, and nodded, frowning at the petulance of the look.

'Oh, I haven't introduced you. Thomas, this is Lieutenant Richard Chute, acting Quartermaster of the 66th. Chute, this is Private Thomas Evans, my secretary, of a sort.'

Tommy glanced at his friend with an amused look.

Chute gave them both an inquisitive look but put it down to the drinking.

'So, Richard, why does the Lieutenant Colonel wish my return so promptly?'

'Have you not heard, then? I don't suppose you would have, really, sitting in the Surgeon Major's tent. The General has ordered us to strike camp and make ready for a march to intercept Khan. He plans to bring him to battle on the morrow.'

Maurice looked as if would fall, so Tommy jumped up and steadied him. Maurice looked at Thomas and then pulled his watch out of his pocket. It was showing 10.45. He looked at Chute. 'When were these orders given, Chute?' he asked in a tremulous voice.

'The orders were officially given at thirty minutes past the hour of ten this evening. I say, Rayner, are you quite recovered, old boy? You look terribly sick.'

'You will have to excuse me, Richard, I am not feeling myself. But rest assured, you can tell Galbraith that I will attend to him shortly. Just a quick rest is in order first.' He turned to Tommy. 'Would you mind escorting me back to my bed for a moment's rest, please, Private.'

Tommy helped Maurice back into the tent and, grabbing the lamp on the way, deposited him on one of the stools and set the lamp on the table. He sat in the Major's chair and waited for Maurice to compose himself.

'How did you know, Thomas? How did you know those orders would be given at 10.30?'

'I've already told you, Maurice, it's in the history books.'

'So that's it, then, is that what you're saying? Tomorrow we're all going to die?'

'I don't know, mate, this is all new to me as well. But as I've said, whether you believe me or not, I don't belong in this time and I have read about this battle. All right, it was years ago, but I read it all the same.' He sighed. 'I don't know all of the facts, I only just managed to get through my A level. But what I've told you already is pretty much right.'

Maurice looked thoughtfully at Tommy. 'Supposing for a moment you are, in fact, some reluctant time traveller, why are you here?'

'Like I've already said before, the last thing I remember is getting hit by an RPG and then waking up here. But I was thinking that maybe I was sent here to stop it, or I dunno, save you maybe?'

'Save me? How preposterous. And how, pray, would you go about doing that running away?

Tommy just stared back and shrugged his shoulders.

'Pah! Well, I can tell you now, Thomas, I will do my duty. And whatever befalls us tomorrow, I shall not be labelled a coward.' He stood in anger and began to pace around the tent. After a moment he stopped and turned on Tommy. 'Is this your way of staying safe, Thomas? Is this some sort of plan to befriend an officer and hope that will keep you clear of the ranks, mmm? Well, I can tell you this, *Private*, I will be at the forefront, standing at the side of Colonel Galbraith, doing my duty. So be warned, if you were hoping to stay clear of any battle, I am one of the worst officers to choose from.' He had buttoned his tunic while he had been talking, and he now placed his helmet on his head, turned smartly and stormed out of the tent.

Tommy sat stunned for a moment, surprised at Maurice's sudden anger. Why had he reacted like that? He wasn't calling him a coward or anything. Then his shock turned to anger. What an inconsiderate shithead! He had just offered the idea that he might be there to save his life, and Maurice throws it in his face, accusing him of being a coward. Tommy went and lay down on his bed.

'I wonder how long it takes to clear a camp this size, anyway, and what the hell am I going to do? Go with them? If I do I'll be killed along with all the rest.' Tommy pondered hard and long into the night, listening to the sounds of soldiers on the brink of a large battle. If he was honest with himself, he was starting to feel a little scared, and dark thoughts were popping in and out of his mind. *What if I die here? Will I truly be dead? If I don't save Maurice, will I have to stay? Am I supposed to change the past? Won't that have an adverse effect on the future or something?*

He recalled the science fiction films that mess around with time travel, and they always said that any changes in the past, however slight, would have enormous consequences in the future. *What was it called?* he thought. *Oh yes, cause and effect.*

'SHIT!' he shouted, 'Why doesn't someone fucking wake me UP?'

'Well, you sound awake already, Private, unless of course you are having another attack of delusions?' Preston strolled in through the tent flap and went straight to his desk. 'I may be convinced shortly, Mr Evans, that you will need to return to Kandahar, and then India, for it sounds like you may be suffering from slight damage to the brain and will need proper care in a hospital. For further tests, of course. What say you to that?'

'I don't need to go to India, sir. I was just thinking out loud, that's all. I am much better now, thanks.' As he finished speaking, Maurice came through the flap with a flourish, followed by Arun. He went straight to his bed and began collecting his personal items, placing them in a trunk at the foot. He studiously ignored Tommy as he packed.

'I say, Major Preston, sir, would you mind terribly if I borrow Arun here to collect my things together and get them stored on the baggage? This trunk is particularly burdensome.'

'Not at all, Lieutenant, please instruct Arun as you will. My orderlies will be here presently to strike the tent and move everything to the baggage train. Mr Evans, you may want to pack whatever belongings you have. I'm sure Arun will also help you.' Preston left the tent shouting for Watson and Holmes.

Tommy chuckled at that. *Very clever*, he thought to himself. *Very good, Watson and Holmes, very good. Dead funny, that.*

'Is something funny, Thomas? Why are you laughing? Have I said something humorous?' Maurice frowned and stared at Tommy.

'No, Maurice, it's not you, it's something the Major said.' He shook his head, smiling, then looked at Maurice thoughtfully. 'Can I come with you, Maurice? I don't know where I'm supposed to be anyway, and it's not because I don't want to be in the ranks. I can handle myself all right, it's just you're my only friend, and, well, we can watch each other's backs if it gets a little rough, you know.'

Maurice became thoughtful, and after a few moments he smiled at Tommy. 'Certainly, old chap, that would be a splendid idea, and I know you can more than handle yourself. It's just that it doesn't befit an officer being seen to mix with the rank and file, no offence. So we will have to come up with a new role for yourself and hope nobody realises that I have stolen you from the lower echelons, what.'

Tommy mused over this for a few moments. 'What about a secretary? You know, what you told that Chute fella. You can have a male secretary in this time, can't you?'

'As opposed to a female? What a ridiculous notion, Thomas, I would not have a female secretary. They are want to gossip, you know. No, that won't do, my dear chap, if anybody would have a secretary it would be Galbraith. But you could be my runner. Yes, that's it, you will be my runner, Thomas, my batman.' He put out his hand for Tommy to shake. 'Do we have a congruence, my dear?'

Tommy shook his hand. 'Yeah, that sounds terrific, me old mate, whatever that is.'

Just then the tent opened and in bustled two soldiers, one of whom Tommy recognised as being Private Watson. They both tipped their hats to Maurice and started about collapsing beds and moving the Major's desk and his various personal items. As Tommy owned nothing but the uniform he was wearing, and was therefore not packing, he approached Watson, who was collecting the Major's case.

'Hello, mate. Remember me?'

'Well, now, that I do, lad. Ye still thinking yer in the navy, then?' he said with a smile.

Tommy smiled back. 'Listen, mate, you know when you found me? Can you tell me what I was doing? You know, was there anything strange about it?'

'Din' I already tell yer this, lad?'

'Yeah, I know, but I had a knock on the head, didn't I, so it's all a bit fuzzy like. About what you said – I know most of it, but did you see anything or anybody, I don't know, strange?'

Watson stood still for a moment, looking thoughtful and rubbing his chin. After about a minute, he said, 'Well, there was that old Bhisti wallah.'

'Bhisti wallah?'

'Yes, lad, an old Bhisti wallah was leaning over yer, chatting away in that heathen tongue o' theirs and trying to rob ye, by look's o' things. But I saw him off. I did, offered him a bit o' steel.'

'And that's all, just a Bhisti wallah?'

'Aye, that's all, lad.'

'Would you be able to recognise him again if you saw him?'

'Ha, they all look same to me, bloody heathens. Now, as enjoyable as this chat is, I 'ave a lot to do, so if you'd be so kind as to 'elp me take this desk out yonder, seein' it's so bloody heavy.'

Tommy nodded and lifted one end and, with Watson on the other, they shuffled outside. Tommy was amazed at the scene and he stood gaping as thousands of soldiers were going about, pulling down tents, bivvies and shifting all sorts of cargo – boxes, stools, chairs, tables, all manner of things. Tommy lifted the desk onto the back of a cart which was already loaded with a wealth of objects, from beds to stools, bedding, boxes and crates. Tommy looked further on from the cart and, in the light from hundreds of lamps and fires, he could see a long column of carts and horses. *A baggage train*, he thought, and he swore he even saw a camel at one point.

'That's a hell of a lot of stores for such a small army, mate. Not exactly travelling light, are we.'

'Aye, lad, it's that bloody commissariat and the extra stuff fer officers. We got too much baggage and we're moving at a snail's pace, and ye don't need to be a General to know that little truth. Jesus and his saints, I can't keep nattering all night, boy, I'll never be done. Good luck and be safe, lad.' With that, he nodded to Tommy and continued to load supplies.

Just then Maurice came out of the tent followed by a heavy-breathing Arun carrying his trunk. 'Please be kind enough to load it with the medical stores, my good man, and make sure my name tag is facing outwards. I don't want any light fingers in there.'

'Yes please, Lieutenant Sahib.' And Arun struggled off to load the trunk.

'Ah, gentlemen, rejoining the regiment, are we?' said Major Preston as he approached the two friends. 'Well, I wish you both the very best of luck in the coming confrontation, God knows we will all need it. Do you know that my request for extra water rations for the men has been totally ignored? I tell you this, these men will struggle to last a day without plenty of water in this infernal heat, and after a long march. Madness, I tell you.'

'My dear Major, I am sure the Brigadier General has thought of all these problems and made arrangements. Not even he would be silly enough to march us off into a hostile landscape without enough water. Now you must excuse me, sir, I have to report to Colonel Galbraith. My thanks for all your care and attention.' He shook Preston's hand and moved off.

Tommy held out his hand and Preston took it. 'Good luck tomorrow, Mr Evans. I wish you well, young man.'

'Thank you for looking after me, sir, and I hope you survive the battle.'

Tommy moved off to join Maurice and was watched all the way by a bemused Major, who couldn't for the life of him understand why the young man's parting words made him shiver. Shaking his head at his own foolishness, he turned to oversee the loading of the medical supplies.

Chapter 9
Battle - *The Beginning*

Tommy and Maurice made their way across a sea of activity, a maelstrom of ordered chaos. Horses whinnying, dogs barking, men shouting orders or telling each other to 'Fuck off', some playful, some serious, but the activity did not stop; it was like a machine. *At a quick glance,* Tommy thought, *you would think that it was a ragtag rabble rather than the cream of a Victorian British fighting force.* But looking closer, he could see the discipline of the ranks, orders being given and followed without question, officers moving in and out of the troops, giving orders here and there, cajoling some, berating others, NCOs shouting at the ones who weren't working quickly enough. Most of the noise and banter was coming from the lines of the 66th, and Tommy could hear a plethora of accents, from Irish to London to West Country.

'Oi, Paddy, move your fuckin arse and get those boxes loaded or I will stick my fuckin' boot up it.'

'Am right on it, Sar'nt, to be sure.'

'Fuckin' bog hoppin' mick.'

'Private BECK! If I wanted you to sit on your arse and watch everyone else working, I would have instructed you to do so. Now stand up and help Private Drew there lift those bloody tents onto that cart, and if I see you sitting down again, you 'orrible little man, you will be cleaning out the khasi with your tash brush.'

'Right away, Colour Sar'nt Gover.'

'Hey Sammy, d'ya reckons Mrs Ashton is keepin busy back home?'

'Feck off, Bolton, least I got a woman, you sheep shagger.'

Tommy was enthralled. Apart from a couple of walks around the camp and the fight with the Grenadier, this was the closest he had come to the lower ranks. And strangely, he felt quite at home. Maurice, on the other hand, was keeping up appearances and looking down his nose under his impeccably aligned helmet. Every soldier they passed tipped his hat in deference, the Sergeants coming smartly to attention. Tommy was aware they were making their way towards a largish tent that had not yet been taken down.

'Thomas, when we arrive at the Lieutenant Colonel's tent, please remain silent unless a question is addressed to you directly. The old man is a stickler for the rules.'

'Right, Maurice.'

As they approached the tent, Tommy could see a group of officers standing around a table. Two he knew, Garratt and McMath, the others he did not recognise. They came to the table and stopped; Tommy, at the rear of Maurice, came to attention while the other saluted.

The older officer, who Tommy took for being in charge, turned to Maurice with a smile and put out his hand to shake.

'Well, it's very pleasant to have you back. Mr Rayner. I have been struggling without my favourite adjutant. You are quite recovered, I hope?'

'I am, sir, thank you. I have been quite impatient to return, but the good Surgeon Major Preston did not agree with the self-diagnosis of my robust, anatomical manifestation.'

The older officer chuckled and swept his hand around the table. 'The officers of the 66th you know, of course.'

Maurice smiled and nodded to most of the assembled officers.

'This is Lieutenant Hector Maclaine of the Royal Horse.' Galbraith indicated to a rather surly looking young officer.

Maurice nodded to him and was rewarded with the briefest of nods in return. In fact, Tommy thought, the artillery Lieutenant's face was in a permanent lofty sneer. It looked as though he was smelling shit or something.

'Who do you have there behind you, Rayner?' And as everyone's eyes turned to Tommy, he straightened up, even more if that was possible.

'Oh, this is my runner and batman Private Evans. The good Surgeon Major had him attached to me until I am fully fit, as it were. He will be my eyes, ears and legs, so to speak.'

'A pleasant evening to you, Private,' said Galbraith.

Another Irishman, thought Tommy. *Why the hell are they called the Berkshires?*

'A very good evening to you, sir,' Tommy barked, parade-ground fashion.

'Eyes and ears you say, Rayner,' snapped Maclaine. 'Is he literate enough?'

'My dear Lieutenant, Evans has a sharp intellect and an enquiring mind. He is more than literate enough, I assure you, but please feel free to question him if you won't take my word for it. Why don't you try to confound him on English, mathematics, geography, languages even. That is if you have any viable, non-horsey or cannon related questions, what.'

Maclaine's perpetual smirk dropped off his face and was replaced with one of anger. There were a few hidden smiles around the table, and even Tommy couldn't help but smile at Maurice's rebuff.

'I say, that smile wouldn't be for me, would it, *Private*?' Maclaine looked at Tommy.

Maurice chimed in suddenly. 'Oh, and I might also add that Evans is the 66th champion, after knocking that big Grenadier about a bit. In fact, he's extremely handy to have around, a sort of intelligent bodyguard, so to speak.'

'I saw that,' Garratt joined. 'That was a bloody good show, Private. Brought some respect back to the regiment and, more important, I won a couple of shillings, unlike McMath here.'

'I am sorry for the lack of faith, Evans, but to be sure that was a big man you were up against, so it was, and I was sure you would come off worse than he.' McMath smiled apologetically at Tommy.

Tommy just smiled and nodded to the two Captains. Maclaine, on the other hand, was watching Tommy with a guarded look under the rim of his helmet.

'Right, gentlemen, back to the business at hand,' interrupted Galbraith. 'You are all now aware that the Brigadier General has ordered us to strike camp and make with all speed to,' and he indicated by pointing to a place on the map which was spread out on the table, 'here…Maiwand.'

Tommy shivered.

'The Brigadier General believes that if we can get there first and make ready, we can surprise the buggers. We can set up our guns to make best of use of them and deploy our infantry in the best possible formation as to cause havoc amongst Ayub Khan's forces. Although they will outnumber us slightly, and have, so the rumour suggests, better guns, we still have the better trained army, and they must not be allowed to reach or bypass Kandahar, to make for Ghazni or Kabul. We are to stop them, or slow them down. Now, there are the native regiments to consider. The Jacob's Rifles are untested, as are the Grenadiers, but they are led by experienced British officers so hopefully we shouldn't have too much of a problem.'

'Those natives can't be trusted. They will turn and run as soon as it gets too hot,' Maclaine sniffed.

I really don't like this twat, thought Tommy. *He sounds just like that arsehole Dashwood, but a hundred times worse.*

'Mr Maclaine, need I remind you not to burlesque the native regiments in front of the men?' He glanced at Tommy. 'They are trained soldiers of Her Majesty, and will accord the same respect as all the regiments out here, including our galloping gunners.'

Maclaine was about to retort when another group of officers approached the table.

'Ah, good evening Oliver. Blackwood, old man, I was just saying to the young Lieutenant here how lucky we are to have your boys behind us.'

'That's gracious of you to say so.' A man of medium height stepped up to Galbraith. (*What's with the gay biker moustaches?*

Tommy thought). 'We look forward to protecting the 66th from all those nasty tribesmen.' They smiled to each other and shook hands.

Tommy was enjoying this posh banter but his legs were starting to ache and he was bursting for a piss.

'I was just giving the final details of Burrows's orders to the officers here. I trust you are also making ready with haste?'

'My chaps will be ready before the sun shows its face. What time do you expect we will be on the march?'

'Sometime around six o'clock, no later. We need to get into position as soon as possible if we are to make an easy day of it.'

My God, thought Tommy, *if only you knew*. He remembered Galbraith now. *Yes*, he thought, *he was the ranking officer of the 66th who was killed. The poor bastard!*

His legs were now starting to ache even more, probably due to that scrap with Singh, and he noticed more officers joining the group at the table. He jabbed Maurice in the ankle when no one was watching, who turned, and Tommy indicated that he needed to go and pee. Maurice nodded.

'Private, go and keep an eye on the chaps and see that everything is moving along. Any problems, speak to Sar'nt Major Cuppage or report directly to myself, understood?'

'Yes sir, right away sir.' Tommy pulled off a smart salute and trotted away back towards the 66th.

As he cleared around the side of a tent, he stopped, undid his trousers and had a much deserved pee.

'Oi! Fuck off, you dirty bastard,' shouted a voice from inside the tent.

Oh shit, he thought, and quickly tucked himself away just as a figure scrabbled out of the tent and came at him with a swing. Tommy just about ducked and stepped away quickly.

'All right, mate, sorry about that, but I was busting.'

The soldier stopped and stared at Tommy. 'I know you, yer that lad who beat that fat ugly bastard t'other day. Hey Billy, come out 'ere and see who we got pissin' up our tent.'

Another much larger man came out of the tent and stood in front of Tommy; he was about six feet, bull necked and had an enormous moustache. His other distinguishing features were his two black eyes. He stomped up to Tommy and smiled, and gave him a bear hug that knocked the breath out of him.

'Put 'im down, Billy, you'll kill 'im. I said put him down.'

'All right, Charlie, keep yer hair on.'

Tommy dropped back onto his feet, struggling for breath with his hands on his knees. After a moment or two, he looked up into the smiling faces of, he supposed, Billy and Charlie. 'All right gents, how are ya?'

'Eh, hear that, Billy? We're gents now. Well, pleased to be making your acquaintance an' all that. The name's Charles Croft, and this here's my associate, William Davis.'

'Sorry about pissing on yer tent, fellas, but I had nowhere else to go.'

'S'all right, chum. After what you did to that bastard Grenadier, well, you can piss in the tent next time, if yer want. I won fifteen shillings on ya. Now what brings you to our neck of the woods?'

'I was told to come down here to see how things were going. Galbraith's adjutant, Lieutenant Rayner, sent me.' Tommy immediately regretted what he had said, as the two soldiers promptly adopted a guarded look.

'Woo, hang on, don't worry about me, boys, I'm just employed as a runner for him. I'm not a grass.' He was rewarded with blank stares. 'You know, a snitch? Backstabber? A tattle tale, then.'

'Ah, right, I understand. So why ya doin' that fer then, how come yer not wiv the lines?'

'It's complicated. I was told to do it for Rayner as he's not fully fit yet, and he can use me to do the stuff he can't, if you know what I mean?'

'Not really,' replied Billy with a confused look.

'Don't worry about our Billy, he's 'ad is 'ead knocked about too many times.

Tommy smiled and looked around, at the soldiers going about their business, loading carts, wrapping rifles – in socks, by the look of it – packing canvas bags with items of clothing, cups, pots and pans. He noticed that there was a subdued feel to the soldiers now; they were still taking the piss, but not to the extent they had earlier in the evening.

'What ya call that boxing then, wiv all that kickin' and stuff?' The noise had come from the monster moustache. Billy had spoken a sentence, a whole one, and he had probably been putting it together since Tommy had arrived there.

'Well, it's called kickboxing, strangely enough.' *My God*, Tommy thought, *no wonder he lost that fight. He has the IQ of a plum!*

'So lads, ain't you supposed to be packing or something?'

'Thought ya weren't no blabber mouth, then,' growled Charlie.

'I ain't mate, but you might wanna start.'

'Oh, aye, and why's that, then?' replied Charlie, as he pulled his waist band higher.

'Oh, I don't know, how about Sar'nt Major Cuppage walking towards us. That good enough for ya?'

'What! Fuckin' 'ell, he is as well. Move ya fuckin' arse, Billy, ya daft apeth.' With that, he grabbed Billy by his braces and dragged him over to a canvas bag and started throwing things in it.

Tommy chuckled to himself as he watched the soldiers panicking, with Charlie throwing curses at Billy who was very nearly tearful. Suddenly he felt a presence behind him, a large one at that according to the shadow that had just fallen over the packing soldiers. Tommy swung round to face Cuppage, came to attention and cracked out a smart salute.

'Hello again, Private. And what brings you out tonight? I thought you were convalescing with Galbraith's adjutant, Mr Rayner?'

'Pleased to report, Sar'nt Major, that myself and Mr Rayner have been declared fit for duty, and I was selected to be Mr Rayners secreta— runner for the coming hostilities. I am to be his eyes and ears, Sar'nt Major.'

Cuppage stepped closer to Tommy, close enough to feel his breath on his cheek. 'There is something different about you,

Evans, something very strange, something I can't put my finger on. We have not met before, yet I find you very familiar.'

Tommy looked back into his eyes and tried not to quiver. This man had an enormous presence and he made it felt at all times. After a moment or two, he stepped back and looked over Tommy's shoulder at Billy and Charlie, who had stopped to gawp at the two men. 'Do not cease in your packing, gentlemen. We wouldn't want to leave two outstanding soldiers like yourselves behind, now would we.'

'No, Sar'nt Major Cuppage,' they chimed together, and continued in their hasty packing.

'I am on my way to speak with the Lieutenant Colonel shortly. Would you care for a stroll through the camp, Private, so as to make a report for Mr Rayner with details of the readiness of the brigade to move?'

'Thank you, Sar'nt Major.'

'Very well, come.' He turned and strolled deeper into the 66th lines. Tommy waved goodbye to Billy and Charlie, who waved back. Well, Billy did and smiled. Charlie stuck his tongue out.

Cuppage talked as he walked and he took such big strides that Tommy had to keep a fast pace. 'So you transferred from the Fusiliers, Mr Evans? How find you the Berkshires since your arrival?'

Tommy was gobsmacked that he remembered his name and nearly stuttered his reply. 'Extremely professional, Sar'nt Major, and highly disciplined all round.' This was all he could think to say.

Cuppage looked sideways at Tommy with a curious frown. 'You are well spoken for a Private, Evans. How is this? Did you attend school fully?'

'Yes, Sar'nt Major, I did all my schooling on the Isle of Wight.' He disclosed this information, hoping the Sergeant Major hadn't been there.

'Indeed. I was stationed at Parkhurst for a time. And how did you learn to fight? I watched you the other day, as I was with the Brigadier General's party. Your style was highly unusual, to say the least, and believe me, I have seen lots of different fighting techniques.

Tommy had to think quickly. 'When I was a boy, Sar'nt Maj—'

'For goodness sake, call me Mr Cuppage.'

'Yes, Mr Cuppage. Like I was saying, when I was a boy, my father owned a small boat builders in Cowes, and he employed a Korean man as a labourer. They and the Chinese worked all over the docks in Portsmouth and Southampton. Well, he taught me a bit of taekwondo, which is the Korean fighting style. I learned it for years until I joined the army.'

'The Hermit Kingdom, eh? I have not been there. Well, you do it very well.'

There was a fuss around one of the carts as they approached some of the cannons.

'I'm telling you, we don't have room for all this ordnance, so you're just going to have to leave some of it.'

'With all due respect, sir, I think we will probably need all of it in the coming days.'

Tommy and Cuppage stopped. The others stopped talking and came to attention, apart from one, who Tommy recognised as Chute, who Maurice had spoken to.

'Can I be of assistance, Lieutenant?'

'Ah, Sergeant Major. Yes you can. Will you please inform Sergeant Rice here that he cannot pack all the ordnance we took from the levies as there is no room for it, and I doubt very much if we would have need of it anyway.' He was red in the face and sweating profusely, even though it had started to cool in the early hours.

Cuppage turned to Rice. 'What say you, Sergeant Rice? Do you think we will need all these shells? Do you feel the horse artillery will not have enough to deal with Mr Khan's army?'

'Sar'nt Major Cuppage, sir, it's my belief that we can do away with cooking pots and bedding and anything of no use in this coming battle. Every shell, shot and shrapnel will be needed, or me and the lads won't be any use if we run out. And besides that, we threw away most of the ammunition when we took these guns off the levies and only have about fifty rounds each.'

Cuppage mused over this for a minute or so, whilst looking over the ammunition cart. Then he turned to Chute.

'That seems to me to be a fair argument, Lieutenant. Might we come to some compromise and make a little more room in the baggage? For as Sergeant Rice has pointed out, if he were to run out in the coming battle, these cannons attached to the 66th would become redundant, would they not? I am sure you will agree, sir, that we could make do with a little less comfort and perhaps a little more protection.'

'Oh, for heaven's sake, very well then. But I will not be explaining why we haven't enough pots and pans to feed the army. You may make some small room, Rice, and that is all, damn your eyes.' He stormed off into the darkness.

'Carry on, lad, and make sure you can squeeze as much ammunition onto those carts as you can, clear?'

Rice smiled and seemed to stand a little taller. 'Yes, Sar'nt Major Cuppage.' He turned and started to shout, 'Allen, Corke, Drewitt, Gilbert, get the rest of that shot on the cart. Basden, Gunney, Lambert, go and find me some galloping gunners and some oss's to shift this lot, and where the bloody hell is McDermott? That 'orrible little shit!'

Tommy watched Cuppage, who was himself watching Rice go about his duties. He had a slight smile on his face. He waited a few moments before Cuppage, not even looking at Tommy, said, 'Do not think too badly of the Lieutenant, Mr Evans, we all have our jobs to do, and some know theirs better than others. And when in time of war and battles and death, always, but always, trust your NCOs to get the job done correctly. Understand?'

'I do, Mr Cuppage, sir.'

He became thoughtful again, watching some of the 66th men loading ammunition onto the carts, and, Tommy thought, he looked a little sad.

'My niece married a man like that fellow Rice, a likable rogue, I'll give you, but a rogue all the same. She is far too good for him and my sister was rather unhappy about their union, for she finds soldiering unromantic and boorish. Her husband is a chemist, you see, a rather dull one, I might add. The girl's husband is fighting for Queen and country in the Zulu lands. A Corporal he is, Sydney Jackson, a man of questionable parentage from Peckham.'

He took a deep breath and a long exhale, and looked at Tommy, who noticed for the first time the green tint to Cuppage's eyes, illuminated from the many lamps and fires. Tommy found himself remembering other eyes that looked similar.

Hang on a minute, thought Tommy.

No way!

Jackson?

'From Peckham, Mr Cuppage?'

'Indeed, and I know not why I divulge this information to you,' he shook his head. 'Shall we continue and you can tell me more of that fighting technique?'

Tommy smiled.

'I would be pleased to, sir.'

And Tommy followed the tall Sergeant Major deeper into the ranks of the 66th.

Sometime after about three in the morning, a tired Tommy walked back up to Galbraith's tent to find Maurice. There was no one about except a young soldier packing things into a large wooden box. He was a private, Tommy noted, so he approached him without worry.

'Hello, mate, have you seen Rayner anywhere?'

'Ye mean Lieutenant Rayner, don't yer.'

The soldier had an insulted look on his face as he replied to Tommy.

'Err, yeah, Lieutenant Rayner, then.'

'Well, he's taking a small repose in that tent yonder,' he indicated this by pointing to a small tent about twenty feet away from Galbraith's. 'But he shouldn't be disturbed, for that's what he told me.'

'All right, mate, no worries.' Tommy then caught a whiff of tea and walked over to a small fire by Galbraith's tent. He noticed an urn hanging over the fire.

'Eh, me old mate, any chance of a chai, then?'

'I suppose,' came the reply from the soldier, and he picked up a cup and filled it with black, unsweetened tea and handed it to Tommy.

He drank deep even though the liquid was burning his throat, and after a few minutes he began to feel revitalised. *That is quality shit*, he thought, *even without sugar or milk*.

'So what's your name, then, mucka? My name's Tommy.'

Tommy thought he looked to be a similar age.

The soldier stopped what he was doing. 'My name is Michael, Michael Darby.'

'Well hello, Michael, and how are you this fine evening?'

He looked at Tommy with a doughty look.

What a fucking stiff, Tommy thought.

'Well, I be fine.'

'All right, Mike, so what do you do around here, then?'

'My name is Michael. I'm a drummer with the 66th.'

Silence!

'Right then I can see that you're a real chatty bloke, so I'll piss off and find somewhere to get my head down.'

The shock on his face was almost laughable, Tommy thought; he turned and made his way to the tent that the drummer said Maurice was in.

Tommy looked about to make sure no one was watching, especially Michael the drummer, who went ahead with his packing, and entered the tent where his friend was supposed to be resting.

Tommy stood over Maurice, who was lying in a camp bed, and not too comfortably, by the look of it. He was talking in his sleep again.

'Victoria, my dear my fair Aphrodite, take off the corset.'

'Victoria, Jane! Maurice, me old mate, are you some sort of gigolo?'

Maurice started, sat up and rubbed his eyes. 'For goodness sake, Thomas,' he croaked, 'that little filly was almost mine,' he sighed. 'A prize I have been trying to reach since a stolen kiss and a handful of teat at a Christmas ball.' He stood, stretched and smiled at Tommy, then checked his watch. 'My God! Is that the time? We must be away, Thomas, we wouldn't want to miss the party, what.'

'I wouldn't mind missing it, mate.'

Tommy shrugged at Maurice's dour stare and then moved to the camp bed and sat. 'Do you mind if I get an hour, at least? I'm knackered.'

'Oh, very well, Thomas, but an hour and no more. I will go and find some breakfast. I shouldn't think we'll be eating again for a while.' He turned and left the tent, shouting for Michael to get some food cooking.

Some time later, Maurice returned and roused Tommy with a cup of steaming tea and a bowl of what looked like porridge. 'I rather think this should be the other way round, old chap, don't you?'

'Cheers, pal.' Tommy sat up and accepted the cup and placed the bowl next to him. After looking around the tent, he noticed it was getting light outside. 'What time is it, mate?'

Maurice retrieved a revolver from a canvas bag and placed it into the holster attached to his webbing. 'It is just after six o'clock, Thomas, so you might want to hurry with that food as we will shortly be on the march.'

'Right then.' He picked up the bowl and started to eat, chewing slowly on the salty porridge. 'That's a nice pistol you've got there, mate.'

'It is a thoroughly ungainly Mark I Adams and it has the stopping power of a smelly fart. It annoys the natives rather than kills them.' He holstered the weapon. 'I might just as well throw it at them; at least then I might hurt one. But it was all I could get my hands on at the time, so to speak.'

Tommy noticed the guarded expression and wondered if he had to supply his own kit. *That would explain it*, he thought.

Maurice sighed as he placed his helmet on his head. 'Thomas, my dear chap, just a thought. Where is your rifle? Come to think of it, I haven't seen you with a weapon since we met, and, yes, I'm sure you consider those fists of yours to be weapons, but unless you can reach a hundred yards, I suggest you acquire one, what.' He picked up a rifle leaning against the table. 'Perhaps you should go and see Chute and see if he can supply you with one. I keep this Martini–Henry for myself, just in case things get a little silly and I have to get my hands dirty.'

Tommy stood and indicated the rifle, which Maurice passed him. He inspected it closely. It was the same as he'd seen in the 66th lines; he didn't know what the Indian regiments were using, but from what he'd seen, they were different. He was surprised at the weight. It looked heavier than what he was used to but it was actually lighter; there was also a bayonet, he noticed, that looked like a bloody spear. Single shot, he mused, with a lever action to eject the cartridge.

'That, Thomas, *does* have stopping power greater than a fart. In fact, it will put lots of holes in Ayub Khan's fair family of fanatics.'

Maurice passed him a large bullet which Tommy placed in the breech. 'So you just close it and it's ready?'

'Pull the lever shut, old chap, and it's ready to drop an elephant, although shooting Ghazis is much more fun I hear. When you release the lever, the casing will be ejected. But unfortunately it does have a tendency to jam every now and then.' Tommy passed it back to him.

'I don't think that Chute fella will give me a rifle, Maurice, not from what I saw earlier. He seems to be a little under pressure.'

Maurice thought for a moment. 'I have a novel idea, then, Thomas. You can have this one, and I won't have to get my hands dirty at all, then, will I?'

He passed the rifle back to Tommy and handed him a wrap of cartridges. 'Just bloody well make sure you're watching my back, old chap. If any of those bloody savages gets through, well, all I will have is my flatulence.'

Tommy smiled and shouldered the weapon. He placed his helmet on his head and nodded to Maurice.

'Ready when you are, me old mate.'

He followed Maurice out to an already brightening day, and the heat was already climbing. Tommy could now fully appreciate just how much work had gone on over the course of the night. The camp was already moving in places; the 66th were drawn up and ready to march in column. The baggage stretched out behind into the distance, and, he was right, there were camels, loads of them, carrying all sorts of supplies. They had Indians riding them or pulling them along, and donkeys, carts and horses everywhere, as well as long lines of Indian infantry, who he thought looked extremely smart.

'Maurice, where am I going to be? Am I going to be with you or what?' He started to feel the enormity of it all and was starting to panic a little.

His friend was walking to a group of officers on horseback, and though he was no judge of horses, these were fine looking beasts. He noted Garratt and McMath were there, as well as a few others he didn't recognise. Galbraith was there, with Oliver at his side. Sergeant Major Cuppage was standing ramrod straight and inspecting the 66th column and the endless NCOs walking up and down the lines, shouting and giving instructions.

'Jenkins, I don't give a damn how bloody hot it is, get that button done up, you shower of shit.'

'Jones, dinna try an' pull that, wee man. I know yer noo sick, but ya will be when a finish wi' ya.'

'Honest, Sar'nt Walker, I feel faint.'

'Och, away, ya wee shite.'

Maurice turned to Tommy. 'I'm afraid, old man, that you will have to walk with the column. It can't be helped, but report to Sar'nt Major Cuppage and tell him I wish you to be at the head, as you are my batman and runner, and do try not to worry so, Thomas. All will be well.' He smiled at Tommy. 'Galbraith has ordered me to be at the front with these men,' he said, nodding to the other men on horseback.

'The main brigade staff will be coming on behind.' He then turned around and mounted a large chestnut coloured horse. He looked down at Tommy.

'We are in a respectable position, Thomas. Along with the cavalry there and a couple of guns, we will lead the brigade forward, you and I, my fearless, futuristic friend.'

Tommy rolled his eyes and saluted, and made his way to Cuppage, gaving him the instructions from Maurice.

'Indeed. In that case, you can accompany myself on this march, Evans, and be sure to have your canteen full, for I fear the Devil himself will be breathing over us today.'

Tommy saw an officer indicate to Cuppage, who then shouted in parade-ground fashion. 'The 66th will march, by the left, march!'

This instruction was given all the way down the column by the different NCOs, and the vast snake started to move forward. Tommy was overawed once again by the spectacle of a Victorian army marching together. *How*, he thought, *could they look so bloody good given the heat and dust of this place?* They looked magnificent, with Cuppage at the head just behind Maurice and the other officers on horseback; the guns of the artillery and the Cavalry were beyond them, scouts and outriders beyond them. It was astonishing.

Tommy fell into step alongside a Sergeant, who was walking behind Cuppage. He noticed a different insignia above the stripes and realised it was a Colour Sergeant.

The man looked sideways at Tommy and frowned. 'What's your name, then, lad? I don't recall seeing you before.'

'Evans, Colour Sar'nt, Lieutenant Rayner's batman and runner. Newly joined in India.'

'Are you now? Well, pleased to meet yer. My name's Colour Gover, Fred Gover, 66th man and boy.'

Tommy smiled, tipped his hat and looked around at the column. He could see the Union flag flying back in the middle somewhere, and what he presumed was the 66th Colours. *This really is fantastic*, he thought to himself, *but it is all going to end in a matter of hours, and I am going to be part of that end*.

After a couple of hours of mulling this over and marching across the rugged, dry, inhospitable landscape, watching the endless cavalry troopers racing back and forth, up and down the column, kicking up dust clouds and presumably giving reports on the enemy movements, the order was given to stop and take ten minutes break and get some water. The Bhisti wallahs were out in force, moving up and down, refilling canteens here and there. *Perhaps Major Preston had gotten through after all*, he thought. The heat was incredible. It must be in the high °70s, early °80s already, he presumed; he could feel his shirt and tunic soaked in sweat, and by the look of others around him, everybody was suffering, though Cuppage was giving a strong impression of being made out of stone.

Tommy was starting to feel morose about the whole thing now. *Why*, he thought again, *am I doing this? What possible reason was there for it? Bollocks!* He came to the conclusion that he was still dreaming and it didn't matter if he tried to stop this from happening; it wouldn't matter if he changed the future by doing it, he had to have a go. As the order was given to prepare, he caught up with Maurice, who was standing by his horse alongside Captain Garratt, and coughed to get his attention. Maurice finished what he was saying to Garratt and turned and smiled at Tommy.

'Thomas, my dear chap, how fair you on such a beautiful summer's day?'

'Fucking hot, mate, and pissed off.'

'Thomas, really, I know it must be dreadfully uncomfortable marching around in this heat but there was nothing I could do. I had to buy this horse in India and he cost me an absolute fortune, and, well—'

'Forget that for a minute,' he interrupted. 'Have you told anyone else about what I told you, you know, about the coming battle?'

'Why on earth would I have told anybody else? I could not see you being carted away back to India and then a lunatic asylum, Thomas, for that is exactly what would have happened. You do recall the words in Preston's journal, of course?'

Tommy was thunderstruck as he realised Maurice did not believe a word of what he had told him. 'After all the things I have shown you, told you, you still don't believe me?'

'I like you, Thomas. You have a tremendous imagination and you tell the most incredible tales, but in the end, tales are what they are.' He placed a hand on Tommy's shoulder and smiled sadly at him. 'Preston said I should pretend to believe what you were saying so as not to make you angry because of the wound to your brain, and that sooner or later you would snap out of it.' He sighed heavily. 'I have come to like you, Thomas, a great deal, in fact. But think! If I were not trying to nurse you back to health, why, how else would you explain an officer cavorting with a ranker? It is simply not done.'

Tommy took a step backwards. *Shit!* he thought. *I am completely on my own*. He looked at Garratt, who was smiling sadly at him.

'The Captain knows of your medical condition,' Maurice said. 'He has from the start, and so have the others. They are all aware that I was trying to nurse you back to health.'

Tommy rounded on Maurice. 'You,' he said and pointed a finger at Maurice, 'are a fucking prick, mate.' He turned to Garratt. 'Has he told you anything of what I've said? Has he? Well? Let me tell you, Captain, what awaits you and the rest of this brigade. You will meet the enemy at Maiwand, your guns will fail, your native regiments will fail, your cavalry will be totally crap and, in the end, it will be just the 66th fighting to the death, over a fucking stupid flag!'

Garratt frowned, took a deep breath through his nose and climbed on his horse. 'I would advise you to retake your position, *Private*, before you say anything else in anger and so put pressure on friendships that have been made.' With that, he turned his horse away.

Maurice mounted also. He looked down at Tommy, shook his head and turned his horse away.

Bollocks to ya, he thought, and walked to the head of the column where he found Cuppage, who was staring at him strangely from under the peak of his pith helmet. Tommy returned to the same place as before, but Gover wasn't near. Just Cuppage, who moved to stand next to him.

'I do not wish to eavesdrop, Mr Evans, but that was an interesting conversation you were enjoying with the young gentlemen. Indeed, your conversation with them seemed overly familiar, even to a point of insubordination.' He looked sideways at Tommy. 'Would you care to divulge the nature of your little chat?'

What the hell, thought Tommy, and so for the next hour, with Cuppage asking the odd question here and there, he recounted the whole tale from start to where they were now.

Tommy finished, and started to laugh at the NCO's silence. 'You see? That's what they thought, that I am as mad as a box of frogs.'

'So you believe this friend of yours to be a relative of mine, and by the sounds of things, still fighting in this God forsaken place?' He pulled out a silver case of cheroots and offered one to Tommy, which he accepted. 'Yeah, his name's Paul.'

Cuppage struck a light and offered it to Tommy. 'I have never read Jules Verne and I cannot say as I would like to. He is French, is he not?'

Tommy nodded and sucked the flame through the end of the small cigar, inhaling the smoke deep into his lungs, and promptly started coughing. After he got his breath back, he turned to Cuppage. 'Very nice,' he managed with a wheeze.

Cuppage took a long inhalation and blew out the smoke. 'They are fine, are they not? A relative of mine sends them to me from Virginia. Much better than the poor quality ones in India.'

Tommy was just about to reply when some Indian sowars trotted up to the officers in front and made a report, but Tommy was too far away to make out what they were saying. They were immediately dispatched to report to the brigade staff in the centre, and after a few bellowed orders the column was brought to a halt.

'Sergeant Major Cuppage, a word if you please,' came the request from one of the officers in front.

'Sir,' he barked.

After a short time the brigade staff came up from the centre; Oliver was there, as was Galbraith and, Tommy presumed, Brigadier General Burrows. Tommy waited in the glare of the sun, surrounded by the mutterings of the 66th, and was feeling apprehensive. *This is it*, he thought, *they have made contact*. He continued to wait, the sweat pouring down his face as he watched different riders come and go, some carrying messages to the other regiments. He also watched as the brigade staff party made their way to the front of the column, crested a small rise and looked through their binoculars. While all this was going on, the wallahs went about their business, filling canteens, while soldiers checked their weapons; he could see some gunners around a cannon, making sure their weapon was ready. Tommy was on tenterhooks; he had to find out what was going on. He saw Maurice standing by his horse and he made his way over. Maurice was checking his saddle bag for something as he approached.

'Private Evans reporting for duty, sir,' he said, and he stood to attention.

Maurice didn't turn around. 'I am sure you could be of more use to Cuppage, *Private*, as I seem to be a bit of, what was it now? Oh yes, a fucking prick!'

'I'm sorry, Maurice, I didn't mean it. I just get a little angry now and then, and besides, I'm supposed to watch your back, remember?'

Maurice stopped and leaned on his horse for a moment. He chuckled and, without turning around, said, 'Welcome back, Thomas. And yes, I accept your apology.' He turned around. 'Well, we have arrived and seem to have found Ayub Khan'*s* army as was predicted, crossing the Maiwand plane and heading for Kandahar.'

'So what are the plans, then? Please tell me we're going to turn around and head back to Kandahar, or maybe collect more troops or something.'

'Whatever for, Thomas? He has only a few regiments of Kabuli infantry and horse, maybe a few hundred Herati infantry. Oh, and some guns, nothing to worry about.'

'Did you not hear anything I told you the other night? There will be thousands, mate, *thousands*!'

Maurice frowned. He looked away and shook his head.

'OK, Maurice, no problem, mate. It don't matter to me anyway, does it, so I'll just go with the flow and see what happens.'

Just then a couple of officers on horseback trotted up carrying the Colours. The first officer climbed down from his horse and approached Maurice.

'Rayner, have you heard? The Afghans seem to have brought some of their friends with them. I have just had it from a Lieutenant in the 3rd Sind.'

Maurice glanced at Tommy and then back at the man. 'What do you mean, Honywood?' he snapped. 'You sound like an excited child, for goodness sake.'

'I have just been told that the Afghan army is a little bigger than what we originally thought. It seems our spies have got their figures wrong.' He swallowed. 'There are thousands of irregulars attached to them: ghazis, horsemen and tribesmen. All in all, so our scouts can guess, twenty thousand! Now perhaps you see why I sound like an excitable child.'

Tommy watched the colour drain from Maurice's face.

'What does Burrows intend to do about it, Honywood?'

'I've no idea, I have only just learned of this myself. Burrows is with the senior officers as we speak, but I would presume we would return to Kandahar for reinforcements.'

Maurice cleared his throat and looked at Tommy. 'Well, we will soon find out, I suppose, what.'

Tommy stood to the rear of the group now gathering around the Colours and tried to be inconspicuous. More minor officers and ensigns had gathered, and were talking animatedly about the situation. A little time had passed when Galbraith, Oliver and several other senior ranks and captains walked through the group, giving orders and instructions.

Galbraith talked with Maurice, and the latter began giving instructions to the various officers, repeating the Lieutenant Colonel's orders. Suddenly the 66th came alive with activity. Tommy watched as cannons were pulled past, escorted by a few of the cavalry; he also noticed that the obnoxious twat Maclaine was with them. Orders were being shouted all down the line, and in the other regiments the Indian havildars were doing the same, instructing their naiks in turn. Horses galloped past, dragging more guns with them, but the baggage, he noticed, was being turned around, headed a short distance away toward a small village they had passed. *Well*, he thought, *we ain't going nowhere, are we.*

Tommy approached Maurice. 'I take it were not going back, then, me old mate?'

Maurice stared at Tommy. 'Well, it seems that your skill for soothsaying is in no doubt, Thomas. And no, we are not going back, we are deploying down onto the plane and are going to engage the enemy after all. We will leave the baggage with a small guard at Mundabad village, and we are to make our way there,' he pointed, 'and make ready.'

He stopped for a moment, took a deep breath and continued. 'We will have some guns as well. I mean, we will also have the smooth bore cannon.' Tommy thought Maurice was talking like a robot, his eyes slightly glazed and unseeing. He was in shock, Tommy realised. He finally understood that what Tommy had been saying all along was right, and it had hit him like a bomb.

'Maurice, you OK, mate?'

'What? Oh, yes, I'm fine. I think!' He moved over to Tommy. 'I should apologise, Thomas, for I have doubted you for far too long. You were indeed correct about the size of Ayub Khan's host. In fact, you have not been wrong about anything, really.' Maurice looked into Tommy's eyes. 'But please, Thomas, tell me the destruction of the 66th isn't so. Surely that must be a mistake? This is an excellent regiment, professional, hardened. How can it cease to be?'

He looks close to tears, Tommy thought, and his heart went out to him.

'It's sheer numbers, mate. The 66th will hold their own when it comes to it, but the others, well, they won't, and that will be the end. But listen, not all the lads will get it. Some make it back to Kandahar, and some of the other regiments too. You might be all right. You could be one of the few who survive.'

Maurice was about to speak when he was interrupted. 'Lieutenant Rayner, sir, the Lieutenant Colonel requests that you join him at once.'

'Thank you Colour Sar'nt Bayne, I will be with him shortly.' Bayne moved off. 'Well, my friend, it seems we're out of time. Will you join me?'

'Wouldn't want to be anywhere else, me old mate,' Tommy said with a smile, and he patted Maurice on the back. 'C'mon, let's go and kick the shit out of 'em.'

They found Galbraith in conversation with Oliver and Burrows; the other officers were Blackwood and somebody Tommy later found out to be Brigadier General Nuttall, who was apparently in charge of the cavalry and guns. There were quite a few other officers, but none paid Tommy any attention as he stood next to Maurice. The conversation was about Blackwood and Nuttall; they would reconnoitre ahead and see what was what. That was the gist of it, Tommy thought, if you can get past all the posh shite!

After a few minutes, Nuttall and Blackwood mounted their horses and, with their escort, made off into the haze. Burrows and Gulliver made their way to the front again, and Galbraith turned to Maurice. 'Well, Rayner, here we are. Is the regiment ready?'

'They are, sir. What are our orders?'

'As soon as Blackwood and Nuttall return and inform us of Ayub's movements, Burrows will issue exactly where he wants the 66th to deploy. I don't think it should be too long tho—'

At that moment, a cannon fired, then another a second later. Galbraith frowned and so did Maurice. Some moments later they fired again. At this Galbraith turned to Maurice.

'Would you mind popping along over yonder, Mr Rayner, and finding out who is firing those guns, and at whom.'

'Certainly, sir.' Maurice turned to Tommy and indicated that he should follow him, and they both trotted off to the sound of the cannon fire. After a few minutes, they reached the foremost units. Burrows and the rest of his staff were looking through binoculars and pointing ahead. Tommy looked and was greeted with a vast, arid plain stretching out into the distant haze, across which, he noticed, ran dry water courses and river beds; the backdrop was spectacular, with mountains and hills against a clear blue sky.

Maurice approached Captain McMath, who was also observing the scene.

'Good morning, Captain, how goes the day?'

'Ah, Rayner. And the top of the morning to you also.' He smiled and nodded at Tommy. 'Well, it started all right, up until I beheld the size of the army to our front.' He pointed to where the haze was just starting to clear a little and the two friends could now see the extent of the enemy's size. Tommy swallowed, for he could see at last the object of his own warnings materialising on the plain before them. It was a horrendous sight. The enemy numbered in their thousands, with horses, foot soldiers and God knows what else. Tommy estimated the main column to be about two miles away and crossing the British front, but before he could think anymore about it, the sound of cannon fire could be heard again, a thunderclap rolling back toward the British forces.

Tommy looked down onto the plain, and about a mile beyond the nearest river bed stood two cannons blazing away at the enemy. While he was staring at this solitary duel, Blackwood and Nuttall came galloping back.

'What are those two cannons doing, Blackwood, why have they engaged?' Burrows demanded.

'Seems Lieutenant Maclaine has seen fit to engage the enemy by himself, General. He has taken two guns up and some Sind horse, so I have had to deploy some more cannons in front of that ravine there to cover them.' He indicated by pointing to where two gun teams were setting up.

Galbraith arrived and watched the spectacle, shaking his head.

Burrows became silent for a moment, and then muttered to himself, 'Damn it all to hell, we could have caught them on the hop.'

Tommy suddenly had an idea and he quickly whispered into Maurice's ear.

'Sir,' Maurice piped up, 'Perhaps if we were to attack now in full, while the enemy is crossing our front, might we not cause sufficient damage and confusion that the enemy would break up, and melt away to wherever they came?'

Tommy knew this was his only chance at changing the outcome. If the brigade were to attack at their own choosing, they might just win the day.

Burrows was mulling this over and Tommy willed him to accept the logic of it. *C'mon, c'mon*, he thought to himself, *think, you fucking old twat.*

'No, I think we have lost the element of surprise. What we must do now is play a defensive role. We will deploy along those ravines there, out on the plain.'

He was looking through his binoculars and pointing to where the farthest cannons were deployed. 'The horse artillery might as well stay where they are in the centre now they have chosen the ground for us. The Grenadiers will hold the left along with the rifles, with the cavalry protecting their flank, and the 66th will deploy there.' He indicated once more by pointing.

'Keeping that ravine and village to their right, the cavalry will again keep their flank.' He paused for a moment. 'I want a couple of companies of Jacob's Rifles in reserve, and I also want a baggage guard. Could you deal with that, Galbraith?' He stopped talking for a while, rubbing his chin, and then had one last look through some binoculars. He let them drop and breathed a heavy sigh. 'That's it, the die has been cast. We will let them break themselves on us. Very well, gentlemen, you have your orders. Please make arrangements for the deployment of the brigade and let us go about our business.'

The officers broke and started to mount their horses, giving orders to their subalterns at the same time. Tommy, standing next to Maurice and Galbraith, was gobsmacked. Even he could see that where the General wanted to place the brigade gave no protection, right out on flat open ground.

'Why the hell would he want to go out in the open against that lot?' he whispered to Maurice. 'Why the hell doesn't he deploy back there by those villages. At least we would get some cover.'

'Thomas, we have had our orders,' he whispered back, but Maurice didn't look convinced either. 'Besides, it won't do to go skulking around and hiding behind garden walls when the enemy are out there, waiting for us to give them a decent trouncing, what.' He still didn't look convinced, Tommy thought.

He followed behind Maurice as the 66th and the rest of the brigade deployed out onto the plain. He watched with a sense of wonderment as the different companies began to wheel and arrange themselves behind the guns, to the right of a couple of Bombay infantry companies. He watched the Indian regiments deploying away to the left; the Grenadiers he thought, looked magnificent and totally controlled. He flinched as the cannon opened up again, firing away at the Afghans at a range of around 1700 yards; he looked for the guns attached to the 66th and found them setting up behind the horse artillery. He also noticed the cavalry away to the left and rear in column formation. *Why? Get them out on the flanks ready to charge.* He looked into the distance and found the Afghan host had stopped crossing their front and were deploying for battle. *What a crock of shit,* Tommy thought. *The stupid old fucker should have slammed straight into the flank of the Afghans, using every gun to shell the shit out of 'em.*

'Dickhead,' he said aloud.

'Sorry, Thomas, you said something?'

'What I said, Maurice, me old mate, is that the General has made a huge, massive fucking mistake. Look over there and you will see a shit load of ragheads on horses – their cavalry, I presume – and there, pointing right at our left flank and nobody seems to give a shit.'

'Just a moment, Thomas,' he turned away. 'Yes, Colonel.'

Crump. The cannons roared again.

'Rayner, get the men lying down behind that fold in the ground there, that should afford us some cover. Inform the rifles they might want to do the same and get a company to keep an eye on that ravine directly to the front and right. It wouldn't surprise me if the sneaky bastards use that for cover.'

'Yes, sir. With me, Thomas.' They both trotted forward along the ranks of the 66th, Maurice passing on Galbraith's instructions as they went. When they neared the furthest company to the right, Maurice approached the officer in charge.

'Captain Cullen, a jolly good morning to you, sir. The Colonel wants that nullah covered in case of flanking.' He pointed to the river bed directly to their front. 'Yours and Roberts's company is to take care of this, as the Colonel believes the Afghans may try and get around us, and into,' he pointed, 'the village over there.' Tommy took a good look around, and noticed how deep the ravine, or nullah, as Maurice called it, actually was. It was directly in front of the village to their right, and, Tommy thought, exactly where the brigade should have deployed. The nullah to the 66th front was also quite deep and could afford a lot of protection to the Afghans if they sneaked around this way. Galbraith knew his business, Tommy thought.

All the while, the guns of the Royal Horse and the smooth bore were blasting away at the enemy; there was smoke was everywhere. *When are they gonna fire back?* he thought, as they opened up again.

Maurice shook him out of his reverie. 'Thomas, old chap, please report to D Company in the centre, and give Captain McMath the instructions from Galbraith to cover the nullah directly to our front. I will be back with the Colour party.'

'What? Eh!'

Maurice smiled. 'Thomas, you are my runner, are you not?' Tommy nodded. 'Well, in that case, get running.' He patted him on the shoulder and walked back to the Colonel's position.

'Fuckin' hell,' he said aloud. 'Oh well, might as well enjoy it,' and he ran over to the rear of the centre company, pushing his way through the lines of soldiers.

'Oi, watch who're you pushing, ya glock or I'll box yer ears for ya.'

'Sorry, mate, just trying to get to McMath.' Tommy said to the man he had just pushed.

'Well, well, look who it ain't. Mr Lardy Da! 'Ere Billy, yon mandrake's back wiv us mere mortals.'

'All right, Charlie, how you doing,' Tommy replied to the soldier now squaring up to him. Then he felt a tap on the shoulder. He turned and was rewarded with the moustache that was Private Billy Davis.

''Ello, Mr Mandrake. Are you coming to fight with us, then?'

'Err, sort of,' replied Tommy. 'I have to see McMath first though, me old mate. Might catch up with ya in a bit.' With that, Tommy pushed his way past to find the Captain.

'Don't worry, chum,' Charlie shouted. 'If ya get bit scared, come back 'ere, me and Billy will protect ya.' Tommy ignored the laughing and made his way to McMath, who he had just seen talking to another officer.

The Captain spotted him. 'Well hello, Evans, what brings you to my company, then? Oh, you haven't been introduced. Lieutenant Hyacinth Lynch, meet Private Evans, hell of a scrapper if there was one.'

Hyacinth!

'Good morning, Captain,' he then nodded to the Lieutenant, who politely nodded back. 'Lieutenant Rayner wished me to convey an order from the Colonel, sir. Your company are to keep behind that fold in the ground,' he pointed, 'to deal with *them*, sir.' He pointed in the distance and noted hundreds of Afghans gathering in front of the 66th line. Well, actually, they had surrounded the brigade in a big horseshoe, but he didn't want to think about that.

McMath turned and looked to where Tommy indicated, and found there were indeed quite a few Afghans about a mile away, gathering for what looked like an attack. He thought this over for a few moments and then turned to Lynch.

'Right, move the men up to that cover, Lynch, and make ready. Keep the boys low, and when that rabble of Ghazis come for us, we'll give them a surprise to be sure. My thanks, Evans, and I pray you keep those fists of yours safe. I fancy trying to recoup some lost monies.'

He held out his hand and Tommy shook it. 'Good luck, sir.'

Tommy turned and hadn't gone fifty paces when he hit the ground with a thump. His ears were ringing and he had a mouthful of dirt as he sat up. *What the fuck was that?* he thought. As the scene in front of him materialised, he heard the shouts and screams and the whinnying of horses. He pulled himself to his feet and picked up his rifle, and saw to his horror a horse, or what was left of it, lying on the ground with both front legs missing; the Cavalry Trooper was lying a short distance away, with his neck bent at a funny angle. *What the hell happened?* he thought again, as a soldier calmly walked up to the horse, pulled out a pistol and shot it at point blank range through the head. He now noticed there were more soldiers and horses from the cavalry column and the Grenadier regiment laying on the ground in different states of distress. He made his way quickly back towards Maurice and the colour party. He drew up to his friend and noticed the dirt on his uniform.

'Orders given as requested, sir.' And then, more quietly. 'What the bloody hell just happened, Maurice? I've just pissed myself.'

'Consider yourself lucky, old chap. Those poor blighters in the Grenadiers just got a taste of Afghan cannon. Those "not so many guns" have just opened up, and by God it was huge!'

The earth rumbled again and a cloud of billowing smoke rolled off the Afghan lines at multiple points, as the thirty-odd cannons replied again. It was staggering, Tommy thought, incredible, noise like thunder and worse; the sound of the shells landing in amongst the Grenadiers and Jacob's Rifles, the men of the Horse Artillery and Cavalry. The sound of meat being chopped in a butcher's shop was all Tommy could think of. He watched in horror at the scene on the left flank: the Cavalry still did not move, even though they were taking casualties; the Grenadiers were hunkered down but that didn't stop the carnage from unfolding in front of him, and the Artillery's response looked pathetic in its reply.

He noticed Burrows sitting on his horse with the brigade staff, watching impassively as the battle unfolded around him. *Cool as a bloody cucumber*, Tommy thought, *just like you see in the movies.*

'Maurice, why don't we move back to that nullah thing and the village? We can get some decent cover from there, mate.'

BOOM!

Another devastating bombardment from the Afghans made him duck involuntarily, and this made Maurice chuckle.

'What the fuck are you laughing at, you twat. Have you seen what it's doing to those Indians? It looks like a fucking meat market over there.'

'Thomas, old chap, it certainly won't do to show fear in front of the men. It will destroy their moral. But if it's any consolation to you, I haven't stopped farting since those Afghan cannons started up, and I daren't move as I think I may have dropped a hard one.'

Tommy looked at Maurice, who looked back, and both started to laugh, so loud in fact that Galbraith looked over with a confused frown and then started smiling himself.

'That's the ticket, gentlemen, keep a brave face in front of the men.' This made the friends laugh harder, and even the soldiers nearest started to smile, until the next salvo landed with a crash and somebody shouted that the General had been hit.

Tommy and Maurice spun around and indeed saw that the Burrows was down. Well, his horse was, at any rate. The General stood, brushed himself down and demanded another horse. 'I can't see a bloody thing down here.'

'Jesus Christ, Maurice, this is madness, sheer bloody madness, sitting here, taking this punishment. We're getting our arses kick—'

'*Here they come!*' went up the shout.

Tommy turned to see a hoard of Ghazis stampeding towards the lines of the 66th.

'Oh, fuck me!'

'Company volleys, set sights for 1200 yards,' came a booming voice Tommy knew, and he saw Cuppage walking down the lines behind the men shouting instructions, which were then echoed by the other NCOs. The men were loading rifles and getting into advantageous positions as they waited for the Ghazis to reach optimal firing range for the Martini-Henry rifles, and which left them out of range for their own weapons.

Tommy saw McMath's company out ahead slightly, and beyond them were men lying on the ground and picking off the Ghazis at a distance. *Sharpshooters*, he thought, *the best marksmen*.

The cannons were still firing and the Afghans were replying as the 66th waited for the enemy; they never ran, but they were making a horrible noise. Most at the front were wearing white and carrying some sort of flags or banners, and every now and then they would stop and fire their weapons, then stick their flags in the ground and, brandishing long knives, they would continue forward. Tommy had a fleeting memory of one standing over him. The Afghans behind were wearing different colours and he presumed these were regular infantry, as they were carrying rifles. The noise they were making was terrifying and it was all he could do not to start walking backwards.

'Steady, lads, steady. Let them come, hold your fire.'

'Our Father, who art in heaven,' someone was muttering.

'Shut yer hole, Grimshaw, or you'll be joining him.'

A sudden shower of dirt over Maurice and Tommy indicated how close a cannon shell had come, and Tommy wiped the dirt from his face while Maurice very calmly flicked a bit of muck off his sleeve. He had to smile at this show of indifference.

'Steady, steady now. *H Company, fire!*'

'*FIRE*.' The company on the left opened up at once; smoke and death went reaching out to the oncoming Ghazis. This was followed by each company firing in turn, all the way down the line.

'Reload.'

'FIRE.'

Tommy was silent as he watched the 66th go to work on the oncoming enemy, the ordered firing, the commands readily obeyed, Cuppage, calm as you like, walking up and down the firing line. He flinched as another salvo landed to his left amongst the Grenadiers and rifles.

'FIRE.'

Crash, went the Martini-Henrys again; Tommy glimpsed through the smoke, and even from this distance he could see the controlled fire was having a devastating effect. There were bodies everywhere, lying in piles, some three or four deep in places. Another crash as the Horse Artillery tried to reply to the Afghans.

Tommy looked at Maurice, who was watching the battle with his mouth slightly open. *So this is your first proper engagement*, Tommy thought, and was about to ask him if he was all right when somebody shouted, 'The General's down again!'

Tommy turned and found Burrows sitting on his arse next to a dead horse with a dazed look on his face. He ran over and squatted in front of him. 'Are you all right, sir? Can I help you up?' Tommy grabbed him under one arm and lifted him to his unsteady feet.

'I say, where has he got to, he was just here.'

'Who was, sir?'

'That bally Lieutenant from the 3rd Sind. I was giving him instructions just now, right this minute, where has he got to?'

Tommy looked behind the General at a horse limping away. In its saddle remained the bottom half of a soldier, his feet still in the stirrups, the top half having been taken by Afghan shot.

'Shit! Err, I think he's dead, sir.'

'Of course he's bloody dead, you idiot,' came a voice from behind. 'I should think his head is halfway back to India as we speak.' It was Oliver astride a horse.

'I say, General, if you keep losing horses like this, we will have to walk back to Kandahar.'

'Ha, I know, I know. Well, I will need another, so if you could oblige, Major, that would be terribly decent of you.'

As Oliver slipped from the horse, Tommy took this chance and ran off back to the colour party and Maurice.

'I say, Thomas, old chap,' he shouted above the rifle fire, 'that was awfully decent of you, picking up the old man. I'm sure you will be invited to all his garden parties and will be dallying with his daughters as soon as we're back in good old England, what.'

'Fuck you.'

'Charmed, I'm sure.'

'Mr Rayner,' shouted Galbraith above the noise, 'would you mind bringing the smooth bore to bear on those religious fanatics over yonder, if you please. Burrows has allowed us use of them and I can see the lads will be running short on ammo before long.'

'Certainly, Colonel, at once. Thomas with me.'

'Thomas, with me, Thomas, with me,' chimed Tommy in a sing-song voice. 'What am I, your dog?'

'You are for the time being, my canine friend. Now heel.' He laughed as he made his way over to the centre and the smooth bore cannon.

They approached the cannon team as they fired again. *I've had my fill of these already*, thought Tommy. *They just make you cough and give you a blinding headache.*

'I say, Sergeant, Sar'nt Rice isn't it?'

'Yes, sir, just a moment, sir. FIRE!'

Crash!

'Yes, sir.'

'Sar'nt Rice, I need you to take two guns and support the 66th. Galbraith's orders, you understand.'

'Of course, sir. Just had orders from the General to assist you. I will bring over the nine pounders right away, sir.'

'Very good. Carry on Sar'nt.'

'Right you are, sir. Right, you 'orrible little shits, you heard the officer. Get these guns to the back 'o the 66th, sharpish. Move, you bastards.'

'All right, Thomas, let us return to… hold on, is that Preston over there?' He was pointing to some dhoolie bearers placing a man on a stretcher. They hurried over.

'Well goodness me it is! My dear Major, whatever has happened?'

'I'm sure you're not blind, Rayner. I have taken a bullet to my back and it's bleeding profusely. That's what all the red stuff is, by the way, my blood. I thought you would have learned something in my tent.' He moaned as he repositioned himself on the stretcher. 'I was trying to remove some of the injured from the front myself.'

'My dear Major, it pains me to see you in distress, after all the noble deeds you did for myself and Evans here. Well, is there anything we can do for you, sir?'

'Yes, there is, tell these dhoolie bearers to hurry up and get me back to the baggage so I can dress my own bloody wound.' Just then they lifted him up.

'Aha, divine intervention, Major. Farewell and good luck.' Preston just gave him a dour stare.

Maurice chuckled. 'Nice to see he's kept his sense of humour, Thomas, what.'

Tommy just shook his head as they both continued toward the colour party, where Galbraith addressed Maurice.

'See you those Ghazis over yonder, Mr Rayner, how they just walk into death with nothing more than antique muskets, jezails and sharp knives? They can't even get in close to use them, yet still they come on.'

'I have no idea, sir. It is something to do with their religion, I believe, not being afraid of death, or something along those lines.'

'Permission to speak, sir?'

There was a loud crash as the nine pounders opened up, and Tommy nearly jumped out of his skin.

The two officers looked inquisitively at Tommy. 'Granted. You have something to add, Mr Evans?' shouted Galbraith.

Tommy had no idea why he piped up. 'Yes sir, well, it's a jihad, I think, sir. And in their religion, if they offer themselves to Allah, who is their God, by the way, and die killing or attempting to kill all nonbelievers or infidels, well, they get to go to paradise and live with a load of virgins for a thousand years or something.'

'Really, Thomas, virgins you say? Well now, maybe they have something. Where do I sign up?'

'FIRE.'

'Hume, fire that bloody rifle, boy or them Ghazis will carve you up, NOW!'

'It won't fire, Sar'nt Guntripp, it's jammed or summat.'

'Clear that bloody breech, boy.'

'I'm out of ammo. Where's the bloody wallahs?'

The shout for ammunition was becoming more prevalent as the battle wore on, and Tommy could see soldiers of the 66th digging deep into their pouches.

'I say, Colonel, I think the Jacob's Rifles and Grenadiers are taking a bit of a bashing. I have just seen a couple of the jawans backing out of the fray.'

'Well, let's just hope that Maclaine wasn't correct in his assumptions about the native regiments, Rayner, or, as you would say, we could be out for a duck.'

Tommy observed the left side of the brigade, and they were indeed taking some stick. So far the cannons seemed to be aimed entirely at them and he thanked his lucky stars that he wasn't attached to the Jacob's Rifles or Grenadiers. The number wounded being brought from the front was increasing all the time, and the lines were being depleted because the jawans who were bringing them out were not going back. Where were all the medical orderlies? He had seen some dhoolie bearers when he had spoken to the injured Preston, but that was it.

Tommy looked past the front ranks of the Grenadiers and could see hundreds of Afghan cavalry amassing. *My God*, he thought, *if they get in amongst them, it will be a blood bath. Oh, for a couple of heavy machine guns and mortars*. He looked at the rifle in his hands and realised this was his only protection against that load of religious psychos. He observed the Cavalry still sitting in column and taking the same punishment as the Bombay infantry. *Why the fuck doesn't he get them out the way and stop using them as fodder?* It was like a turkey shoot. He could feel his anger building rapidly at the stupidity he was witnessing.

He looked back to the lines of the 66th and saw, with a sort of satisfaction, that Galbraith was using his regiment's rifles to full, devastating effect, and the mad Ghazi attack had slowed to a stop; they were either turning back or going to ground.

'Thomas, old chap, would you mind awfully going to find Chute? We are running desperately low on ammunition and water, and for some reason the wallahs are nowhere to be seen. We need to get the men replenished as soon as possible.'

'Righto, Maurice, I'm on it. Where would I find him then?'

'Try with the baggage nearest to our positions, Thomas, they should be the water and ammunition stores. I honestly don't know why the Bhisti wallahs aren't out and replenishing the men already…' He was staring towards the rear with a frown.

'I'll go and have a butcher's, mate, won't be long.' Tommy turned and jogged off toward where he thought the supplies might be, ducking and flinching every time he heard the cannon roaring or the massed ranks of rifles opening up. There was smoke everywhere, and the smell of bonfire night. *Idiot!* He tried to spit but he found his throat was parched and he could only imagine the discomfort the soldiers must be in.

The wounded were everywhere now; nearly all Indian infantry, hobbling away to the rear or being treated by comrades on the floor. There was a cart toward the rear and it was here that he found Chute, observing a Corporal handing out leather waterskins to some Bhisti wallahs from the back of a cart.

'Lieutenant Chute, sir, Lieutenant Rayner would like to know why the ammunition and water is not getting forward.'

'Would he, by Jove. Well perhaps you could carry some for me, Private, eh? Go on, help yourself.'

Tommy frowned at Chute. 'Why are you being like that, me old mate? There's no need to be a twat about it, is there? I'm only passing on some instructions.'

'How dare you address me in that tone, *Private*. Apologise at once or I will have you on a charge.'

Tommy walked up to Chute and stood nose to nose with him; to his credit, Chute didn't flinch at all. Tommy remembered what Cuppage had said.

'Listen, pal, the lads back there are gonna have a fucking shit time soon. They are either gonna drop from dehydration or they're gonna run out of ammo or both, so unless you wanna tell the General why the 66th can't fight, I suggest you get to it pronto.'

'I second that,' came a voice from behind Tommy.

Tommy spun and found an officer standing in front of him, staring at Chute. 'And, this is not the first request for water and the relevant ammunition for my Sniders.' He shouldered past Tommy. 'My chaps didn't even break their fast or fill their canteens before we marched this morning, and with the hammering they're taking from that bastard Afghan cannon, they're fighting on will power and sense of duty alone. So, as the Private said, get some wallahs out to the front and restock my men, or my regiment will not last long.'

The involvement of the Grenadier officer seemed to get through to Chute, who, Tommy was sure, was doing everything he possibly could.

'I am trying to get the supplies out, but damn it, all the wallahs are refusing to go near the front, bloody cowards. But leave it with me, Whitby, I will liaise with Captain Dobbs and see what I can do.'

The Grenadier Whitby, a Lieutenant, Tommy saw, nodded and made to walk away; he stopped a few paces away from him with a curious look on his face.

'Satan's cock! It is you, ain't it? How the hell did you beat my man in that fight?' Smiling and shaking his head, he walked back to the struggling ranks of the Grenadiers.

Tommy watched him go for a moment, watched the shells landing amongst the Indian infantry and the Cavalry, the 66th on the right with their controlled volleys, the smoke, the noise and the steadily growing numbers of wounded and dead. A picture of hell. He watched the whole scene with a sense of detachment, of not truly belonging in this nightmarish world; not wanting to be here but now unwilling to leave without seeing all of it. And he couldn't leave without Maurice; he had to help his friend, but didn't know why or how. He turned to

Chute, who was talking to another officer of the commissariat. He grabbed a Corporal and gave him orders for water and ammunition to be taken to the Bombay infantry lines, and after that to the 66th as soon as he could manage. The corporal saluted and ordered a group of wallahs to accompany him. Tommy walked over to Chute.

'Excuse me, sir. I apologise for my comments earlier. I did not mean any disrespect, please forgive me.'

Chute looked at him for a moment. 'All right, well, let's forget all about it.' He gave a stiff smile. 'Good luck to you.'

Tommy smiled, saluted and turned back toward the 66th Colour party; he was halfway there when he saw Arun, running about carrying a leather water skin. 'Arun, me old mate,' he shouted above the noise of the cannon fire. 'How are ya?'

Arun stopped and bobbed his head to Tommy. 'Getting water for soldiers, Private Sahib. You are wanting refreshment, yes please?'

Tommy checked his canteen and found it was nearly empty, so he held it out for Arun to fill. While he did this, he asked Arun if he had seen Preston and if he was all right.

'The Surgeon Major Sahib is being wounded and he is with the baggage.' They both ducked involuntary at another scything volley from the 66th. Tommy was about to ask Arun another question when a shout went up that the enemy were in the rear. Tommy craned his neck to see. There was far too much smoke about, but he was sure he could hear the reports of rifles near the baggage. He could also see small ponies flittering through the smoke, and wondered if that was the Cavalry or the Afghans.

'Arun, I have to get back. Stay safe, me old mate, OK?' He clapped the wallah on the shoulder and turned to make his way back to the Colour party. At that moment, a figure ran through the smoke at him, swinging a curved sword aimed at his head. Tommy just manage to duck; he felt the blade pass through his hair, lost his balance and tumbled over onto his back, looking at the figure above him now attempting to bring the blade in a downward slice at his head. At the last second, he awkwardly lifted his rifle and blocked the blow with a juddering clang. As Tommy attempted to scuttle backwards, the sword came flashing again, but it dropped out of the figure's hand. The turbaned attacker fell to his knees screaming and, as Tommy watched in shock, he fell forward onto his face, with Arun clinging onto his back, repeatedly stabbing him between the shoulder blades with a small knife. After a few moments, the figure went still; Arun stood and wiped the small knife on the Afghan's robes.

'He is not being very nice man, Private Sahib, yes please.'

Tommy stood shakily and looked at the wallah with a sense of wonderment.

'Thanks, mate. He was gonna do me for sure. I owe you one.'

'It is being my pleasure, but Private Sahib should be being more careful on his journey.' With that, he gave Tommy a knowing smile and trotted off into the smoke.

What's he on about? Tommy thought. *What did he mean, journey?* Something was niggling at the back of his mind, but the thought was interrupted as the noise level seemed to intensify all around him, and for a fleeting moment he found himself standing alone with cannon and rifle smoke billowing around him. *Fuck this*, he thought, and turned again for the 66th lines. He reached them a few moments later to find Galbraith in an uproar and bellowing at his subalterns. Tommy moved to Maurice's side and plucked at his sleeve.

'What's the craic, mate?'

Maurice turned to him with a confused look. 'Speak English, Thomas. The Colonel is in a frightful temper. Some Ghazis have gotten into the rear and are engaging Major Ready's baggage guard. They have also managed to infiltrate that village to our right, and the 66th are taking casualties from the buildings and walled gardens.'

There was another explosion from the direction of the Cavalry and the Grenadiers.

'Why on earth are those poor bastards just sitting there on their horses, Maurice? They're just getting picked off. Why doesn't the General move them?'

'Yes, I can see your point, old chap, but it's not my place to reason. Besides, we have our own problems at the moment. Yes, Colonel,' Maurice said, turning away from Tommy.

'I need to know what's happening in that village, Mr Rayner. Get yourself over there and bring me a report, would you please. Oh, and tell Sar'nt Major Cuppage to attend me also.'

'Yes sir. Thom—'

'Yes, I know, "Thomas, with me".'

As they moved off, Tommy noticed the noise from the Jacob's Rifles and Grenadier companies was getting louder, and he realised that they were finally engaged proper, but with whom he didn't know. The noise from the baggage area also indicated a significant scrap was taking place. *Shit!* Tommy thought as he remembered the Ghazi that Arun had killed. If they have gotten round the back already, then shit was gonna hit the fan shortly.

'What time have you got, Maurice?'

'Why, do you have to be somewhere, old chap?' Maurice replied as the 66th fired another massive volley. 'It is a little after noon, Thomas.'

Jesus! It felt as if they had been at it all day and yet it was only a couple of hours, if that. He looked over the lines of the 66th, wondering how the hell they could keep this up in this heat. Then he remembered what the Lieutenant of the Grenadiers had said about what they were going through out on the left flank. *My God! They must be nearly finished.* He had started to notice more and more of the Jacob's Rifles moving to the rear, and pointed this out to Maurice.

'I know, old chap, they seem to be struggling somewhat. I have just heard they haven't many British officers left commanding them. All dead or injured, apparently.'

Tommy thought about this as they walked. 'You do remember what I told you, don't you, Maurice? About how this whole thing falls apart? Perhaps you should go and inform the General that if he doesn't do something about them soon, then they will break up completely.'

'*FIRE.*'

They both ducked as the smooth bore let loose. 'And what, pray tell, do you expect he will say when he hears the tale you told me, Thomas? I would like to keep some credibility in this battle, you know.'

'Then ask Galbraith to point it out to him, advise him or something, make up a fucking story if you have to, just try and get the General to see reason.' Tommy was shouting now, and drawing curious glances from the rearmost troops of the 66th.

Maurice wiped the sweat from his face with his sleeve and took a big sigh. 'All right, damn you, I will talk with the Colonel and try and get him to talk to Burrows about the native infantry, but that is it, Thomas. I do not wish to talk about this again, do you hear.' He looked at Tommy sternly, who knew there was nothing else he could do.

The two friends were approaching the outer companies when Maurice stopped.

'Sar'nt Major Cuppage,' Maurice shouted, and Tommy saw the big man standing with Captain Cullen. He looked up and made his way over to them. And he still looked impeccable Tommy thought.

'How can I be of service, Mr Rayner?' Tommy noticed he was carrying a rifle.

'The Colonel would like you to attend him, Sar'nt Major.' Maurice nodded and made his way over to Captain Cullen.

'Very good, sir.' He turned to Tommy. 'And how find you the battle, Mr Evans? Is it as you were expecting?'

'Worse, Sar'nt Major.'

'I gave your tale some thought, Mr Evans, and it seems to be playing out as you described.' He looked over towards the battered Cavalry and Indian infantry companies. 'So either you are a highly intuitive young soldier and have a gift for military strategy,' he looked at Tommy again, 'or the end is upon us.'

Tommy gave him a sad shrug. 'You either believe me or you don't, sir, but everything I told you is happening. Look around you, the Grenadiers have taken too much stick, the Jacob's Rifles are shitting themselves and won't last much longer, there isn't going to be any Cavalry soon, but your General is still thinking he can win the day.' Tommy shook his head. 'Someone needs to talk sense to the man and get him to pull back towards the baggage and the cover of that ravine and village.' He pointed towards where the baggage was. 'At least you might be able to hold it and you will have your supplys to hand, you know, water and ammo and stuff.' He looked Cuppage in the eyes. 'I'm telling you now, sir, this brigade won't last much longer.'

Cuppage took a deep breath in through his nose. 'Well, let us see what the Colonel wants with me. Mayhap I might try and give him your advice, eh.' He smiled, nodded and walked off toward the Colour party.

Tommy watched him go, then went to join Maurice, who, along with Cullen, was lying below a ridge in the ground and looking toward the village beyond the nullah.

'How many do you gauge there are, Captain?'

'I'm not sure, Rayner. Could be ten, could be a hundred, probably a bloody thousand. But either way, Quarry has had to deploy some of the baggage guard against them.'

Tommy looked and could see little puffs of smoke from the building windows in the village and the walled garden areas. There was also some smoke from what looked like an orchard on the other side of the village, and he could see khaki-clad soldiers lying amongst the boulders and grass, returning fire. Quarry's men, he presumed.

'Very well, Captain, I will tell the Colonel that the village has been occupied by the enemy, but Quarry is attempting to have it cleared, yes.' He tipped his hat to Cullen and backed away from the ridge.

'Follow me, Thomas.'

They hurriedly made their way back but, as they neared, Maurice stopped and stared out toward the front of the 66th lines with a horrified look on his face. Tommy stopped and followed his gaze, and although he too was horrified, he had been expecting something like this. About 500 yards in front of the 66th, thousands of Ghazis rose up as if out of the ground, many carrying banners and flags that fluttered in the wind.

'Where the fucking hell have they come from?' muttered Maurice.

Tommy was more shocked to hear his friend swear than what was in front of him, and he started to laugh.

'What the bloody hell are you laughing at, Thomas, you mad fool?' He didn't get an answer, though, as the call went out all along the 66th line to make ready. Officers were shouting, NCOs giving the same instruction with a bit more colourful language.

'Check those cartridges, lads.'

'Keep those breeches clear, boys. You don't want any jamming with that lot coming at us.'

'Set sights for 400, and remember to aim low.'

'Dina worry boot them bastards, lads, they're all wearing dresses anyhoo.'

'*Fix bayonets.*'

Tommy looked up and down the 66th ranks and was humbled at the bravery of these men, who were standing in front of that mass of madmen out there with nothing but an antique rifle and some coarse language. He saw Captain Garratt at the front of his company, sword in one hand and pistol in the other, leading from the front.

'Come, Thomas,' said Maurice, and he walked off towards the Colour party. Tommy followed. On arriving he heard Galbraith talking to Oliver. 'Well, it will not do, Charles. If those native boys break, our flank will be wide open and that will be the end of that. It will not matter if my regiment are holding, they cannot hold front and rear.'

'I understand, sir, but the General has ordered the Grenadiers and the Jacob's Rifles to hold their positions. There is nothing for it but to hold as best you can.'

'Where is Burrows now, Charles?'

'He's over with Mainwaring and Anderson, trying to shore up the gaps in the Bombay Infantry. How, though, I don't know.'

'All right, then, we will continue to hold here.' As he said this, the 66th opened up on the Ghazis now attacking their front, and the officers turned in unison to watch the proceedings.

'This will get worse, Charles, you've seen the size of the enemy host. They can do this all day. We, on the other hand, cannot; we are already running short on ammunition and water, but that will not matter at all when they throw themselves at us completely, and they will, to be sure. I am starting to believe that we will be lucky to live through this day.' He paused and looked at his feet for a moment. 'I have just been talking with the Sar'nt Major and he is of the same mind, that we should retire to the village with the baggage to make our defence. I always listen to my senior NCOs, Charles. So would you be so kind as to make my request to Burrows that we withdraw while we still have the chance?'

Oliver nodded his head. 'I will, sir, right away.' With that, he mounted his horse and made off through the smoke towards the Grenadiers.

Good old Cuppage, thought Tommy. *He got through to him.* He turned to Maurice, who was watching the Ghazis attack the 66th lines. Tommy watched as well, and saw Captain McMath holding his sword aloft, then slashing it downwards. His company fired a volley on that manoeuvre alone. He tapped Maurice on the shoulder to tell him about Cuppage when he heard Lieutenant Honywood exclaim, 'My God, sir, the guns!'

Chapter 10
Battle - *The End*

Tommy turned to look where the Lieutenant indicated and saw the gun teams of the Royal Horse Artillery frantically pulling the cannon out of the fray.

'What in blazes are they doing?' said the Lieutenant. Tommy heard Maurice call Olivey. 'Bloody cowards.'

'Mr Rayner, would you please go and enquire as to why we have lost the Horse Artillery,' shouted Galbraith above the noise.

Maurice stepped forward with a look of incredulity on his face. He turned to Tommy.

'With me,' he said, and started running toward the gun teams.

'Jesus fucking Christ, Maurice, hang on,' panted Tommy. *Damn, this heat is sapping my strength.* He caught up with Maurice as an enormous volley from the ranks of the Grenadiers crashed out; he looked for the Bombay Infantry and saw that they were now hand to hand with hundreds of Ghazis and regular Afghan Infantry. Tommy stopped to watch, momentarily fascinated by the brutality of the way the Grenadiers were fighting: stabbing, hacking, bludgeoning with their rifle butts. But still the ordered volleys were sending death and destruction to their front. The officers, what was left of them, were still shouting commands, the NCOs still pushing their men forward. *What a sight!* he thought. He tore his eyes away and looked for Maurice, and found him talking to an NCO of the Artillery, so he ran over.

'Blackwood's down,' the Sergeant shouted to Maurice. 'We've lost two guns. Maclaine was overrun, so Captain Slade ordered us to pull back, replenish and reposition.'

Maurice was nodding and ducking every now and then as some shot flew over their heads. 'What state are the Jacob's Rifles in, do you know?'

'They are going to break, sir, very soon, I should think.'

Tommy looked to where the Rifles were positioned to the left of the Grenadiers, and to the right of where the guns had been. *Shit! They're going to go any fucking minute*, he thought. Loads of them were looking backwards towards the cannon, looking for a way out.

'Maurice,' he shouted, 'we have to move, mate. That lot are gonna bolt shortly and I don't fancy getting caught out here on our own.'

Maurice looked at the situation for a moment. 'You speak very wise, Thomas,' he said, turning to the NCO. 'Good luck Sar'nt Mullane.' He tapped Tommy on the arm and indicated for him to follow, back to the Colour party.

'Well, Thomas,' shouted Maurice breathlessly above the noise of battle, 'seems you were right on the mark with your predictions of disaster. I think perhaps you should load that rifle, what.'

Thomas pulled a round out of his pouch, pulled open the cocking lever and pushed it into the breach of his Martini-Henry. Then he removed his bayonet and connected it to the rifle barrel. *Strange*, he thought to himself, but he felt a whole lot better with the extra foot or so of steel. He watched Maurice remove his service revolver and check to see if it was loaded, and the two friends made their way back to Galbraith's party, just in time to see a commotion from the very right of the line, and hear the sound of cannon fire. Tommy took in the unfolding scene. The 66th were heavily engaged with the enemy to their front, but were keeping up an intense fire on them; the Grenadiers were fighting hand to hand with Afghan regulars and Ghazis, as were the Jacob's Rifles, who were being slowly pushed back. The Artillery had withdrawn to resupply, but had lost a couple of guns and a whole load of horses. *Well*, he thought, *what a total fuck up!*

As this thought entered his head, a very young officer came trotting up on a horse from the right of the line. Tommy didn't recognise him, though Maurice called out a greeting.

'Barr, old man, how goes the day with you?'

'Could be better, I suppose, Rayner. The Afghans have moved some cannon up towards that nullah back there, about two hundred yards to our front, but luckily Roberts's boys have sorted them out a few times and they seem to be keeping their heads down some. I say, what the devil is happening over there?' He was pointing to the left flank.

'Good god, the Jacob's Rifles have broken,' exclaimed Maurice, and indeed, as Tommy watched, the steady stream of Indian Jawans turned into a stampede as the soldiers looked for somewhere safer than where they were. They began to roll down and into the rear of the heavily engaged Grenadiers, who were struggling anyway without the Infantry now packing into their ranks. The void they opened to the left of the guns was rapidly filling with screaming Ghazis, stabbing spears and slashing Khyber knives at any unfortunate soldier left behind.

Any wounded soldiers on the ground were horrifically slaughtered by these religious fanatics; in a frenzy, they cut, hacked and stabbed at anything in their path. Tommy moved over to the rear of the Grenadiers to observe this route. *Well*, he thought, *you don't get to see something like this very often*. He watched with a sense of morbid curiosity as a Grenadier was dragged out of the front by these madmen, his turban was ripped from his head and his scream cut off as a broad curved sword chopped and hacked through his wind pipe, muscle and cartilage until, finally separated from his neck, his head was held up like a trophy.

Tommy was horrified, and he felt slightly sick at this spectacle; his only consolation was that, as the Ghazi was about to throw the soldier's severed head back into the British ranks, a huge Grenadier sprang forward, slammed his rifle butt into the face of a Ghazi on his right, fired the rifle from the hip into the groin of another on his left, and finally stabbed the rifle bayonet in a great upwards swing at the Ghazi head hunter, taking him under the jaw. Tommy watched in awe as the bayonet ripped through the back of his head, toppling his turban. The mighty Grenadier was back in his own line before the man hit the ground, still holding the unfortunate soldier's head. *Wow! You only get to see that in the movies.* And then he recognised the big Grenadier as he turned, shouting encouragement at those around him. *Well, well*, thought Tommy. *Singh!* He was still sporting the swollen nose that Tommy had given him.

'Thomas, what are you doing? You're supposed to be with me, remember? Good God!'

Tommy was listening to Maurice, but was also looking toward the oncoming enemy. He raised the rifle Maurice had given him, aimed and blasted a screaming Ghazi straight in the face at no more than twenty feet away; the lead bullet took half his face off. The recoil and power of the rifle surprised Tommy.

'I must remember to pull that in tighter to me shoulder, mate, that really kicked.' He said this while rubbing at it.

'My goodness, that was a hell of a shot.'

Tommy reloaded. 'Yeah, well, it's not over yet, mate. Take a look at that load of mad bastards.'

Maurice watched the deadly melee taking place. 'I don't think our brave Grenadiers are going to hold them too long, Thomas, and I do believe the smooth bore have just been overrun. Bloody hell, I must report to Galbraith, come on.' He turned without waiting for an answer, and Tommy followed, all the time watching the struggling Grenadiers. He was a few paces behind and very nearly got tumbled by the rush of Jawans running for the supposed safety of the 66th rear.

'Arseholes,' Tommy shouted at them as they passed. He reached the Colour party as Galbraith was issuing commands.

'I want the rear ranks of F and H Companies wheeled and brought to bear on those enemies who have broken through. Mr Barr, could you relay my instructions to Beresford-Pierse, if you please, with haste.' He turned to Maurice. 'Rayner, have you seen the General, or Nuttall?'

'I'm afraid not, Colonel. Do you require me to locate them, sir?'

Galbraith became still for a moment, looking towards the now-turning rear ranks of F and H Companies. 'Mr Rayner, locate Burrows and tell him that I believe it is time to retire to the safety of the baggage and Mundabad village. Tell him I cannot hold my line now that the Bombay Infantry have broken.' Tommy watched him give Maurice a sad look. 'Be quick now, Mr Rayner, and be sure to take your batman with you.' With that he turned away, shouting for Cuppage.

Before Maurice could speak, Tommy shouted, 'Come, Maurice,' smiled and ran off towards the rear.

After a few minutes of searching, they located Burrows and other senior officers trying in vain to shore up the break in the lines. Burrows was furious. He ordered Nuttall and his Cavalry to charge and break up the oncoming Afghans, and the Horse Artillery to engage as soon as they were replenished.

Nuttall addressed Burrows: 'General, the Artillery has taken a beating.'

'I couldn't give a fig what state the Artillery are in, damn you. Get them back into action before all is lost. And where is that bloody Cavalry?'

Maurice skidded to a halt in front of Burrows. 'Beg to report, General. Colonel Galbraith sends his compliments and must inform you that he cannot hold the line much longer. He respectfully requests that the retire be sounded and he can withdraw the 66th to Mundabad village and the baggage. He will make a defence there, sir.'

'Does he, by God.' The General lifted his head at that moment to watch the Cavalry grouping to make a charge at the Afghans. 'Come on Nuttall,' he shouted, 'give it to them, and spare ye not the horses, damn you.'

'General, do you have a reply for Colonel Galbraith, sir?'

'Hold your tongue, Mr Rayner. Let us see if this charge breaks that heathen horde.'

What a posh twat, Tommy thought, *sitting on his fat arse while men are dying out there.* He, along with Maurice, watched two columns of Cavalry break into a gallop aimed at the nearest Afghans, who were attacking the fleeing Bombay Infantry.

The noise was fantastic, he thought, the rumbling under foot incredible.

'They're attempting to form square,' Maurice shouted, indicating the Grenadiers and the Jacob's Rifles on the left flank, but Tommy had no idea what he meant, so he just watched. And after a moment or two, he shouted back to Maurice, 'They don't look very square to me, mate.'

'The idiots are attempting regimental instead of by the company. It won't work. They're too fractured.'

'Well, that sounds impressive and all that, but they still look like shit. The Cavalry look decent though, I must admit.' Tommy watched the two lines charge at the Afghans, but at the last minute the right-hand column veered off to the right without engaging.

'Damn them to hell,' shouted Burrows.

After a few moments of dodging galloping horses, Tommy watched Nuttall return to the General.

'Why have you not charged, sir?' he demanded. 'Reform and charge again, damn you.'

'I cannot get the men to obey, General. They will not listen to orders.'

'Will not listen!' thundered Burrows. 'You were leading that charge, sir.'

'That may be, but I will retire the Cavalry to the guns and reform there.'

As Burrows, Tommy and Maurice watched Nuttall trot away to the rear, Major Oliver rode up hard and came to a skidding stop, his horse nearly colliding with Tommy.

'Dickhead.'

Oliver stared at Tommy for a few seconds and then looked at Burrows, 'Well, I think it's fair to assume, sir, that we cannot hold, and I believe we should withdraw.'

As Burrows made to reply, the noise level from where the now-collapsing Grenadiers were still fighting tooth and nail suddenly increased as the very last of the Jacob's Rifles folded under the pressure and began running fully down the lines of the 66th.

'God damn it all, Oliver, sound the retire.'

The Major spun his horse around shouting for a bugler, and Maurice turned to Tommy.

'Well, Thomas, I am returning to my regiment. I give you leave to do what you will.'

'Fuck off, you twat, I'm coming with you.'

They both laughed and made a run for the 66th Colours, dodging running Indian Infantry on the way. They got there just in time to see F and H Companies open fire from both front and rear as the ring of Afghans was tightening. But the mass of fleeing Indian Infantry was making it impossible for the 66th to properly engage. Before Maurice had time to shout to Galbraith, a bugle was heard sounding the retreat, and Galbraith ordered his regiments bugler to do the same. He started issuing orders to the officers for an ordered withdrawal to the village by the ravine. The 66th bugler sounded off, and Tommy could hear the order being shouted all down the line by the NCOs.

Maurice tugged Tommy's sleeve. 'You may want to stay with me now, Thomas, I should think this is going to be a little challenging.' He pulled out his service revolver and started to laugh. 'Well, at least I'm armed. I have my flatulence, what.'

Tommy smiled, but not for long, as the Grenadiers started pushing through the ranks of the 66th. The confusion and terror was electrifying; the once-solid ranks of the 66th were now becoming fragmented as they fell back. Tommy stayed with the Colours as the regiment started to fall back across the plain towards the rightmost village opposite the baggage. Maurice was there, as were the Lieutenants charged with the Colours, Olivey and Honywood; all were firing at the enemy with their revolvers.

He could hear the NCOs shouting for ordered volleys by the company, but Tommy could see what the Bombay Infantry had done to the regiment. Why the fuck didn't they just run to the rear? Why did they have to run in to the 66th? *Terror makes you do strange things*, Tommy thought, and these young Indian soldiers had been experiencing it all day. No water, no food and hardly any sleep had turned these disciplined soldiers into frightened children, and they were looking to the 66th for protection as you would look to a big brother. But on this occasion, he thought, even big brother's gonna get a proper kicking.

Tommy looked to where they were headed and just managed to see Cullen's company, now struggling with the fleeing soldiers. He looked for McMath but could not see him. He looked for Garratt and found him limping along, his NCO holding him up, and he was still firing his pistol into the ranks of Ghazis. Tommy could now see ranks of Afghan Infantry and Cavalry, all bunched together for the kill. He saw Cuppage. *My God, he still looks immaculate, even in this shower of shit*. He watched dumbstruck as the big Sergeant Major reached forward and pulled back a young soldier who was being dragged into the mad throng of Ghazis. One of them jumped at him, but the Sergeant slapped him, a bloody slap! And he fell unconscious to the ground, to be trampled by his brethren.

After what seemed like hours of trekking over the plain under constant fire from the Afghans – though it was actually less than half an hour – the Colour party came to a stop, surrounded by men of the 66th who were firing constantly at their attackers. He realised that the Ghazis were unwilling to get too close to the men of the 66th, the rifle fire being what it was, and they seemed to be attacking the Bombay Infantry more, who, to be fair were offering their backs a lot more freely. Tommy knelt for a moment and took careful aim at a particularly big, ugly bearded Ghazi. He braced the rifle into his shoulder and fired at the man's torso, and was pleased to see him fold up and disappear into the crowd.

'Have a bit of that, you arsehole! Maurice, why have we stopped, for Christ's sake?'

'We have reached the nullah, and it's a bloody deep one at that.'

Tommy looked down the side of the ravine and saw that the place where they had ended up was at least fifteen feet deep. He looked along the channel and saw soldiers sliding down to the bottom. *Shit! We're gonna have to move along or drop down here*. He looked around at the scene. The 66th were still attempting to engage the Afghans with concerted and disciplined fire, but a lot of the Bombay boys had gotten in amongst them and were hampering the British regiment. Small knots of men were fighting back to back as the screaming whirling Ghazis hacked and stabbed and died, but still they came on. There was dust everywhere, kicked up by Afghan horses and the heat was intolerable. The noise of rifles, jezails and now, Tommy glimpsed, Afghan cannons was shattering, and Tommy watched as the cannons were dragged up closer to the British ranks, firing case shot with devastating effect.

Tommy could see men of the 66th, caught out in the open and dying, fighting with bayonets fixed, hand to hand against the Khyber knives; it was harrowing for Tommy to watch. To think that just a few hours ago these men were laughing and joking back at camp. He saw a couple of lads from the 66th, back to back, keeping a circle of Ghazis at bay with their bayonets. It would be mere moments before they were overwhelmed. He recognised one, the old Private with the guitar.

'Bastards.'

Without a thought, he jumped forward, pushed his way through the throng and charged the group of mad Ghazis.

'Thomas, where are you going?'

He ignored Maurice, the anger overtaking him now, and the first Ghazi to react got a bullet straight through the gut, followed by eight inches of Tommy's bayonet. Another lunged as he pulled his rifle back, and this one was rewarded with a straight high snap kick to the jaw and he landed on his arse. He reacted just in time to dodge another sword aimed at his stomach and danced to the left, stepping forward and headbutting the man straight on the nose, enjoying the sound of breaking bones. His helmet was now askew, so he ripped it off. It was on him again, the anger, the need the lust; he couldn't help it, it just enveloped him. He wanted to kill, and he wanted to tear these dirty, smelly bearded fanatics apart.

'Come on, you bastards, c'mon. I'll fucking kill all of ya.' He kicked the knee out from another Ghazi, who went down on his hands, and Tommy laughed as he brought his rifle butt down hard on the man's skull, feeling the bone give way under the impact. He stumbled forward and realised that another Ghazi had made a slash at his back, but his webbing had taken the blow. He spun around, dropping to one knee and shoved the bayonet up into the man's groin. The scream that came from his mouth was animalistic, and Tommy smiled as he stood and rushed forward with the man still pinioned on the bayonet. He stopped suddenly and placed a boot on the man's chest, kicking him off the blade and into a group of Afghans who had now backed away from Tommy's wrath. He was breathing heavily now, but still the anger and desire burned in him.

'What are ya waiting for, ya bastards. C'mon, all of ya.'

The Afghans warily surrounded Tommy in a circle, none willing to be his next victim; all were Ghazis bar one, who was an Afghan regular, armed with a Snider rifle, and he now stepped forward with a smile on his face. He raised the rifle to his shoulder and pointed it at Tommy, not eight feet away.

'C'mon, do it, you fucker.' He was screaming now, spittle flying from his mouth. He heard the report of a weapon and braced for impact; it never came. The Afghan's left eye and most of his cheekbone exploded outward onto Tommy's feet. The man crumpled to the ground.

Maurice was standing right behind him. 'Well, don't just stand there, run.'

Tommy realised this might be his only chance to get out of the situation and promptly ran at the nearest Ghazi. Screaming, the man fell back in terror and Tommy jumped over him, using the man's head as a spring board. He reached Maurice and they both moved back towards knot of men surrounding the Colours. Tommy was walking backwards and nearly stumbled over the body of a man from the 66th. It was the guitar owner. He stopped to look down at him; he had a bullet hole in the chest. He also had a strange smile on his face, Tommy thought.

'That was a mightily stupid and incredibly brave thing you did, Mr Evans,' Galbraith shouted over the noise.

'Remind me never to get into an argument with you, young man.' He smiled at Tommy.

Tommy surveyed the scene. He couldn't see much with all the bodies in the way, but what he did see was a couple of hundred men fighting around the Colours, using it as a focal point.

'Right, gentlemen, I think it's time we moved down into the village,' Galbraith said. 'Colour bearers, with me,' and he slid down the nullah on his arse.

'Come on, Thomas, no more heroics, eh? I wouldn't want to have save you again, what.' He slid over the edge of the nullah. Tommy followed, as did the Colour party and most of the men around him, including a lot of Grenadiers who were still fighting gallantly.

Tommy reached the bottom and looked left and right along the dry water course and saw men everywhere, alive and dead, individual duels and battles. The lads from his regiment were not giving ground easily and Afghans were suffering terrible losses in their eagerness to destroy the 66th. He saw a horse limping along the nullah; it was McMath, surrounded by what was left of his company, and Tommy thought he looked in a proper shit state. His left arm was hanging down by his side; it looked to be nearly severed and he wondered if it had been cannon fire. He jogged over to him and stopped them man from nearly toppling from his horse.

'Ah, Mr Evans, thank you, thank you.'

'You should get that arm seen to, sir. Why don't you ride to the baggage and get the Surgeon to take care of it?'

'Do you know what, Mr Evans,' he said hoarsely, 'my friend Ernest Garratt fell before we reached this ditch. He had already been shot about the legs and yet still he rallied his men before he took a bullet to the head. Do you know, I think I fancy staying here with my men a little longer. To be sure, I don't think they will cope without me, and besides, I like the view.' He laughed and started coughing, and Tommy could see he had lost a lot of blood.

'Now I do believe you are Rayner's batman, are you not, so I think you should be with him and the Colour party. Me and my boys will hold this lot off for a little while yet. Now go on, off with you boy.'

Tommy choked at this. He gently took McMath's hand and said goodbye. He turned and trotted over to where the Colour party were reaching the outer part of the village. As he neared them, he couldn't help but look back to McMath, but the horse he had been mounted on was riderless, surrounded by the remnants of D Company fighting to the death.

'Thomas, come on, we must away,' shouted Maurice. But as he was groping his way up the other side of the nullah, he felt hands grab his ankles and drag him back down. He turned as he crashed to the bottom and was rewarded with the snarling face of a Ghazi brandishing a long knife. *Shit!* He realised he had dropped the rifle on the way down. Without thinking, he jumped forward and slammed his fist into the mouth of the Afghan, removing some of his teeth in the process, but as he connected, he felt something collide with the side of his own head and he stumbled down onto one knee. He looked up, dazed, to see an Afghan regular about to strike him again, a rifle in his hand.

'Oh shit!'

At that point, an arm circled around the soldier's throat from behind and pulled him backwards and down, whilst the other hand was punching a knife repeatedly into the Afghan's kidneys.

'There ye are, my little darlin', have a little bit of that, ye heathen bastard.'

Tommy was dazed, but he could see that the soldier who had just saved him was one Private Charles Croft, aka Charlie.

'Well now, who do we have 'ere. Then. Oh, it's Mr Lardy Da,' Charlie said, as he lowered the now-murmuring Afghan to the ground. 'This is not a friendly place to be, chum, best we fucked off somewhere, eh?'

Tommy's head was clearing. *Jesus*, he thought, *that was quite a knock.*

'After you, Charlie, me old mate.'

'Best follow me, then Lardy Da, this way and pick up yer fuckin' rifle.'

Charlie moved off toward a less steep incline of the nullah. The two men had to duck from the pot shots the Afghans were taking at them, but they made significant progress until Tommy realised that some of the shots were coming from the village they were trying to reach. 'Hang on, Charlie, if we climb that now, we'll get picked off at the top.'

'What the 'ell are yer on about, we 'ave to get to that village, chum. It's where all the other fuckers are headed, aint it?'

'There are fucking ragheads in the village, *chum*.' Tommy instantly regretted saying this. 'Look, mate, look at the smoke coming from those gardens.' He pointed. 'They are Afghans in there, and if we climb now, we're dead men.'

Charlie was looking round like a cornered rat. 'What we supposed to do, then, eh? Tell me that.'

Tommy looked around frantically and saw a chance. A group of Bombay Infantry were about to crest the nullah a little further on. *This is our chance*, he thought. *They will draw their fire*. It was wrong to think that way, he knew, but it was every man for himself now.

'Get ready, Charlie.' He gripped his rifle. 'GO,' he shouted, and sprang up and over the lip of the nullah, feet scrabbling in the dirt and rocks for purchase. He turned and dragged Charlie up by his arm and they both made a run to the nearest building. But halfway there, Charlie skidded to a halt, staring at a group of Ghazis attacking a lone soldier of the 66th, who was only just managing to fend them off with his bayonet.

'Billy,' he shouted, and started running at the nearest Ghazi.

Tommy skidded to a stop. 'Oh fuck it,' he said, and started after Charlie, who had already reached the group of men and was laying into them with his bayonet. By the time Tommy arrived, two were already down, having been stabbed in the back, and Charlie was on the back of a third, a stocky man, and was trying to throttle him in a choke hold. Tommy launched himself at one of the others and stabbed at him with his rifle, but this one was no novice, and he parried Tommy's bayonet with his knife. He backed off, and the Ghazi, with a face full of hate, charged at him, swinging wildly with his blade at his face. Tommy leaned back out of the way and swung his rifle around like a club, catching the man with enough force to put him over.

Seeing his chance, he jumped over him and stabbed the bayonet down into and through the Ghazis white robe, through his chest and out the back into the dirt. It was a killing shot and the man died instantly. But the blade was well and truly stuck in the ground and in the man's ribs.

'Shit, c'mon you twat,' he shouted, as he put his foot on the man's chest and tried to pull the blade free. While he was doing this, he checked to see that no one was attacking him. That was when he heard Billy Davis shout in anger and saw him running toward Charlie and the big man he was fighting. The blade finally came free with a squelch, and he ran forward to where Billy was making a sort of grey porridge out of the big Ghazis head, or what was left of it. Tommy moved over to Charlie, who was in a foetal position, clutching his stomach. He gently moved his arms away and saw that the Ghazi had opened his gut, and he was trying to stop the contents falling out. 'Shit, fucking shit,' Tommy shouted.

Charlie was shaking. 'Oh, what a bastard he was, big fucker. Look after our Billy, eh?'

'You can look after him yourself, mate, we just need to—'

But Charlie's head slumped sideways to the ground, and Tommy, after a few seconds, closed his eyelids.

He stood and found Billy staring down at his friend. 'I'm not leaving ya, Charlie, not for this heathen to hurt ya anymore.'

'Billy, we have to move, mate, c'mon. He's gone and we have to go.'

'You had best be going then, Mr Mandrake,' the moustache rumbled. 'I will stay and look after our Charlie.'

Tommy was in a predicament. He badly wanted to go but he couldn't leave this big stupid oaf on his own, so he stood, loaded his rifle and watched as another group of Ghazis made their way towards him. He lifted his rifle and took aim at the nearest, catching him in the chest. He pulled the lever, expelled the casing and loaded another cartridge, fired and took another one through the shoulder. But when he tried to expel the casing, it wouldn't budge.

'Shitting hell!'

He frantically cocked and uncocked the lever, but the casing would not move. He looked at the Ghazis stalking him. He looked behind and then looked at Billy, who, Tommy thought, was smiling again, his moustache bending up at the ends.

'Bye bye, Mr Mandrake.' And with that, Billy gave a powerful roar and ran at the Afghans, smashing them apart like bowling pins. Before Tommy could do anything else, Private William Davis of the 66th was swallowed up in a crowd of screaming bodies, slashing and stabbing. He disappeared from view.

Tommy stood rooted to the spot. He couldn't believe what the big man had done, and was overwhelmed with pity and gratitude. He wished he had never called him an oaf. Rifle fire broke through his reverie and he looked to the sound. It was the Colour party away to the left being engaged by Afghan regulars.

'Shit! Maurice.' Tommy dropped the useless rifle and ran towards the Colours.

The little group of soldiers surrounding the regimental and Queen's Colours was significantly reduced, Tommy thought, and was still moving backwards, firing all the time. They were still at the side of the nullah, not far from where McMath had fallen, and were not far from a small street with walled gardens on either side. Maurice was still there firing his pistol. Tommy grabbed a rifle from a dead soldier as he approached him.

'Thomas, old chap.' He stopped, took aim and fired. 'Thought I'd lost you, old man, you have been missing all the fun, what.'

Maurice was covered in dirt and his helmet was missing, but he still managed to be dignified.

'Yeah, well, I had some of my own, thanks.' He loaded his rifle, which he noticed was covered in blood, and shot at the nearest Afghan. 'Why the fuck are we still here, Maurice? Let's get going.'

'Thomas, my dear, it won't do for me to leave the Colonel. As you can see, he is injured.' He fired his revolver again.

Tommy looked to where he indicated and could see that Galbraith was on one knee and firing his pistol. The Colour bearers Olivey and Honywood were still with him, but Galbraith was holding the regimental Colours. Honywood looked as though he was sporting a wound to the leg. There were a number of soldiers surrounding him, as was Sergeant Major Cuppage, who, Tommy noticed, still looked as though he was on parade.

'Maurice, if we don't move pretty sharpish, we ain't getting out of here.'

Just then a shout went up, and Tommy turned to see Galbraith lying on his back. *Shit! That's that, then.* He looked around at the other soldiers, thinking they would start running, but to his surprise they stood, and more came and stood around the body of Galbraith. *What the hell is wrong with these people?* he thought. *Why can't they just pack up and leg it?*

Honywood picked up the Colours and started waving them back and forth, shouting something Tommy couldn't hear. He was also drawing a lot of attention from Afghan rifles. What a dick!

The whole party began to move down the garden-lined street. Tommy followed Maurice, ducking every now and then from the bullets and shot whizzing by like wasps. Tommy spied a couple of Afghans moving at the other end of the street, so he knelt on one knee, sighted on the first man, fired and put him down. He quickly ejected the spent cartridge, loaded another and took aim. *This is a fucking brilliant gun*, he thought, as he fired and nearly took the leg off the second man. 'Did you see that, Maurice? Now that was shooting, hey, Maurice,' he turned. 'I said did you—'

Maurice was leaning against the wall of one of the enclosures, and for a moment Tommy couldn't understand why his friend was taking a break, until he noticed a large red stain spreading out from his right shoulder.

Tommy dropped his rifle and dropped to his knees. 'Shit, Maurice, you hit, mate?'

Maurice was staring ahead with a look of pain on his face, his breathing shallow and extremely fast. Tommy quickly undid the buttons of his tunic to look at the wound; he gently pulled his shirt apart and saw the ragged gaping hole in his friend's chest. Tommy couldn't breathe for a second; he knew enough about battlefield triage to realise this was a killing wound, even in the twenty-first century. He couldn't look Maurice in the eye, and felt tears prickling his own; he looked away and started to slam his fist into the mud road.

'You fucking bastard. Fucking, shitting bastard, arghhhh!'

'Thomas, old chap,' he wheezed, and Tommy could hear a rattling sound coming from his chest, 'I wouldn't damage those things, you know, they're worth far too much money, what'.

Tommy stopped and became silent, tears running freely down his face.

'Thomas, I know the wound is grievous, I cannot focus my eyes properly and I am feeling rather cold.' He coughed then, and a globule of bloody sputum dribbled out of his lips.

Tommy looked him in the eyes and could see them dimming slowly. 'Maurice, I can't help you, mate, the wound's too bad. I, I can't, I, sorry, I'm so sorry.'

'Perhaps now I can look my father in the face, what,' breathed Maurice.

Tommy stifled a sob.

'All will be well, Thomas,' he coughed. 'Our paths must now separate.'

The sound of rifle fire was building in the background, and Tommy turned to see Cuppage near a garden, holding onto the Queen's Colour.

'You must save yourself, Thomas. I never listened to you, and you were telling the truth.' He coughed again and nearly lost his breath. 'You don't belong in this place, Thomas and you must flee while you can.'

'I won't leave you, Maurice, not now, mate. Not after all we have come through.'

Maurice turned his head. 'Look there, Thomas, Sar'nt Major Cuppage is gone.'

Tommy looked to see the Sergeant Major propped up against a wall, his chin forward, resting on his chest. *He looks asleep*, Tommy thought, *and so dignified, even in death*. There wasn't a mark on him, but a single small hole on his left breast. He watched the last of the 66th and a few Grenadiers retreat into a garden, back to back, and he spotted Lieutenant Henn with them. *Well, he's not such a twat after all, then*, he thought.

'Do you see, Thomas? Please go, it will bring me some peace knowing you got out. And besides,' he smiled, 'I might get to see some virgins, what.'

'I will stay with him.'

Tommy looked up to see drummer Darby standing next to him, carrying a rifle with a bloodied bayonet. He looked back to Maurice, reached out and grasped his hand in both of his. 'I am proud to have met you, Maurice. I will never forget you.'

Maurice smiled back at him and nodded. 'Go,' he whispered.

Tommy stood, turned and, without looking back, started walking to the other end of the village. He wiped his eyes and loaded his rifle. As he neared the end, he stopped and turned to look back; he couldn't see Maurice or Darby anymore, but he did see the last of the Colour party charge out of the garden, standing back to back, firing at the Afghans who dared not come too close. And they started falling one by one. He couldn't watch the rest and walked out of the village.

As he cleared the outskirts, he saw the rest of the brigade fleeing up the road toward Kandahar. *What do I do now?* he thought. The movement of Afghan Cavalry made his mind up for him, and he ran toward the rear of the trail of refugees. Before long he came upon a Ghazi struggling with an Indian native; the Afghan had a knife at his neck. Tommy stood over the Ghazi and slowly, deliberately, pushed his bayonet into his kidneys. The man screamed and rolled over. 'That's for Maurice, you prick. Die slowly, you mad bastard, and give my love to Allah.' The Indian jumped up, breathless.

'Many thanks, Private Sahib, yes please.'

'Arun!' Tommy nearly burst into tears.

'It will be most important, Private Sahib, for to be running now.' He turned and sprinted towards the rear of the column.

Tommy turned and saw what made Arun bolt. Afghan Cavalry were charging down on him, heading for the fleeing brigade.

'Oh, fuck me!' Tommy ran, dropping his rifle. *Well*, he thought, *what use will it be against that lot*. He could feel the ground shaking as they drew nearer, and he looked ahead for deliverance, which came in the form of the Royal Horse Artillery, who were unlimbering two guns. As Tommy watched, he could feel the hairs stiffen on the back of his neck. *They're aimed at me*, he thought, and as this popped into his head, two clouds of smoke appeared ahead of the guns. He could have sworn he saw something moving very fast at him.

When asked later in life what it was like to get hit by a cannon round, he said it was like getting hit by an RPG.

Tommy lay on his back with the wind firmly knocked out of him, like someone was sitting on his chest. *Bugger*, he thought, *I'm gonna die, again!* All the noise started to fade away. No cannon or rifle fire, none of that incessant stupid screaming from those Ghazis. *This ain't too bad*, he thought, as the clouds started to drift lower. *Think I might just have a quick nap*. He closed his eyes and heard a faint voice. He opened his eyes slightly; they were so heavy. He saw the face of Arun hovering above him.

'You had best run, me old mate, I'm dead anyway. Go on, get going,' he said weakly. He was drifting again, but then Arun spoke.

'Please do not be worrying, Private Evans Sahib, I will be coming with you on your journey, yes please.'

'Eh?'

Then darkness.

Epilogue

Pain. Shocking, teeth-clenching pain so bad that he thought his head was going to burst. He tried to open his eyes but found that they were being held shut. Something was across them and was wrapped around his head, keeping them closed. He tried to speak but nothing came out, and he tasted blood on his tongue. He tried to move, but found himself held down in a sitting position; an extremely uncomfortable position at that. *What the hell is going on?* he thought. He lifted his arm to touch his face. *Uurgh!* He recoiled at the touch. *What the hell is wrong with my hands?* He investigated a bit further and without seeing he realised he was wearing gloves. *Gloves! I don't recall wearing gloves, why am I wearing gloves?* He could hardly hear himself think; the noise around him sounded like a high speed train, and he thought he must be in the middle of a storm because the wind was tearing at his face. He tried to speak again after clearing his throat.

'Arun.'

Nothing, just the sound of a gale blowing.

'Arun, are you there mate?' he shouted.

'Don't worry, pal, we'll be home shortly.'

Who the hell was that? he thought. He lifted his hands to his face and tried to remove the cover over his eyes. 'Goggles! These are goggles.' He dragged one of the gloves off but at that moment his stomach jumped up into his throat and he felt violently sick. He vomited and felt it slide up his face, into his nose; and then he was thankful he was wearing goggles.

'What the fuck,' he screamed, as he felt himself becoming weightless.

'Hold on, pal.'

Weightless! 'Yes,' he shouted. He was in an army chopper; they had finally picked him up and he was going back to base. It was all a dream, all of it; Maurice, Arun, Preston, all of them. Cuppage, McMath, the battle. He started to cry, real chest-wracking sobs. 'All a dream.' He can go home now, be back with his mates, back to reality.

Tommy swiped at his nose and tried to open his eyes again; he managed it this time but still couldn't see for all the vomit over the goggles. *This is a bloody bumpy ride*, he thought.

'Are we taking fire, mate?' he shouted.

'You could say that, old boy, yes.'

What a typical snotty RAF pilot, he thought to himself, *university type, better than all the rest. Twat!*

'Now hold on. We're going down and this might get a little bumpy. I think I've lost the landing struts.'

'Landing gear, you mean! What the hell hit us, a ground-to-air?'

'I haven't the foggiest idea what you're on about, old girl, but if you mean that maxim the Afghans were firing at us, then yes.'

'What! Eh?'

'Listen, friend,' the voice shouted, 'if you can't take a joke, then you shouldn't have joined.'

Tommy was utterly confused again. 'Joined what?'

'The Royal Flying Corps, you idiot. Well, not now, actually it's the Royal Air Force as of last year, when the Great War finished. Anyhow, hold on to your false teeth. This is going to be a little bumpy.'

'WHAT!'

'Brace for impact.'

Tommy screamed, long and loud all the way down, as the Royal Air Force BE2C biplane headed for the ground.

Acknowledgements

T here are many references to and different perspectives on the battle of Maiwand, so it was a bit of a slog, albeit an enjoyable one. *My God Maiwand! Operations of the South Afghanistan Field Force, 1878–80* by Leigh Maxwell is a must-read for anyone interested in further exploring the second Anglo–Afghan war, and there is an abundance of material online, including the Berkshire's memorial site: www. roll-of-honour.com/Berkshire/ReadingAfghanCampaign.

The characters I have used are based on real people, and although I have given them personalities of my choosing and used plenty of artistic license, I have endeavoured to keep them all in the best possible light. But, with any fictional story, it is always good to have a few 'bad guys'. Some of the characters I have made out to be incompetent or of a boorish nature, as with the Grenadier boxer, a bully turned hero. Any offence given is unintentional, as I believe the men who took part in that disastrous battle were heroes. The language and slang in the book was typical of the time, and indeed is still in use today by certain individuals, and I used it to give more authenticity to the story.

As interesting characters go, Sir Arthur Conan Doyle based his Doctor Watson on Surgeon Major Preston, and there were indeed two men named Watson and Holmes attached to the 66th Foot.

A great big thanks to my family who have put up with me whilst writing this book. Their patience and encouragement was greatly appreciated.

The second book in the series, *Flying the Colours*, will see Tommy transported not home, but a few years into the future to the 3rd Anglo–Afghan war of 1919, where he will meet yet more interesting characters from the past, including a certain young RAF officer named Arthur Harris...

Richard Thomas